THE DEVILS OF DIRT TRACK RACING

DEDICATION

To the dirt track warriors, the unsung heroes who pour their hearts and souls into the pursuit of checkered flags. May this story honor your grit, your passion, and your unwavering dedication to the sport we love.

PREFACE

The roar of the engines, the smell of burning rubber, the thrill of victory – these are the elements that define dirt track Late Model racing. It's a sport that captivates the senses, ignites the adrenaline, and pulls you into a world where the stakes are high and the competition is fierce. But beneath the surface of the high-octane thrills lies a darker reality, one that's hidden from the casual observer.

This is the world of "The Devils of Dirt Track Racing," where ambition fuels deceit, where alliances are forged and broken in the blink of an eye, and where the pursuit of glory comes at a heavy cost.

This book delves into the shadows of the sport, peeling back the layers of deceit, betrayal, and desperate ambition that lie beneath the surface of the glamorous facade. It's a story of broken dreams, shattered relationships, and the lengths people will go to in their relentless pursuit of ultimate
victory.
Get ready for a wild ride.

INTRODUCTION

Welcome to the heart of the dirt track, where the smell of gasoline and the roar of the engines are the symphony of life. This is a world where the ground shakes with the thunder of horsepower, where the air crackles with tension, and where every turn of the wheel is a gamble.

"The Devils of Dirt Track Racing" isn't just a story about a sport; it's a story about the people who live and breathe it.

It's a tale of drivers and crew members, their lives intertwined in a complex web of ambition, desire, and desperation.

We'll meet them all: the seasoned veterans, the hungry rookies, the passionate spouses, and the loyal crew members.

Each of them driven by their own motivations, their own dreams, their own demons.

This story is a journey into their souls, a glimpse behind the curtain of their lives. We'll witness the highs and lows, the triumphs and tragedies, the love and the betrayals that define their existence.

Prepare to be swept away by the raw power of this gritty, high-stakes world, where the line between passion and obsession blurs, and the pursuit of victory becomes a dangerous obsession.

THE ROAR OF ENGINES

The air hung thick with anticipation, a palpable energy that crackled in the humid summer air. The smell of gasoline and burnt rubber, a heady mix of danger and excitement, filled the senses. It was a Friday night at the local dirt track, and the heart of Late Model racing was about to beat with the roar of engines and the thunder of tire smoke.

The grandstand was packed, a sea of faces illuminated by the bright lights that spilled out onto the track, their eyes fixed on the brightly colored cars lined up in the pit lane. The drivers, clad in fire suits that seemed to be an extension of their own skin, were a mix of seasoned veterans and eager rookies, each one driven by the same insatiable thirst for victory.

The roar of the engines swelled as they revved, the sound a primal scream that sent shivers down your spine. The announcer, a man with a voice that could make the dead sit up and take notice, started the countdown, each number echoing through the packed grandstand.

"Five… four… three… two… one… GO!"

The green flag dropped, and the cars erupted in a chaotic ballet of speed and precision. Tires screeched as

they surged forward, throwing up clouds of dirt that momentarily
obscured the scene, only to reveal a kaleidoscope of color and motion. The rumble of the engines was a symphony of power, each car a symphony of steel and fire, vying for a coveted spot in the lead pack.

The track was a tight, twisting ribbon of dirt, with banked turns that seemed to defy gravity. The cars slid and swerved, their drivers maneuvering with a mixture of skill and daring. The air vibrated with the thrum of engines, the smell of burnt rubber intensified with each passing lap.

The crowd roared with every move, every near miss, every bold pass. There was a palpable tension in the air, a collective heartbeat that quickened with each lap. This was no ordinary race; it was a battle of wills, a contest of skill and nerves, where the line between victory and defeat was razor thin.

It was a world of intense competition, where the drivers were not only battling for the checkered flag, but also for their place in the pecking order. The drivers, both young and old, were hardened by years of struggle and sacrifice. For them, this was not just a race; it was a way of life, a chance to prove their worth, to leave their mark on the dirt track.

As the race unfolded, rivalries flared, alliances formed, and the tension thickened with each turn. This was a world where lines blurred, where morality was a luxury that few could afford. It was a world where the only rule was to win, and the means to achieving that goal often took a backseat to the relentless pursuit of the checkered flag.

The excitement was palpable, the tension thick enough to cut with a knife. It was a world where dreams were made and broken, where fortunes could be won and lost in the blink of an eye. It was the world of dirt track Late Model racing, and it was a world unlike any other.

It was in this world, amidst the dust and the roar, that the story of the Devils of Dirt Track Racing was about to begin.

MEET THE CONTENDERS

The air crackled with a charged energy, a potent mix of anticipation and gasoline fumes. The smell of burnt rubber hung heavy, a familiar aroma to those who lived and
breathed this world. The roar of engines filled the air, a guttural symphony that vibrated in your chest, shaking your very core. Beneath the bright lights of the dirt track, the gladiators of this sport, the drivers, awaited their turn to battle.

This was their stage, their proving ground. The roar of the crowd, a sea of faces lit by the reflections of the neon lights, fueled their drive. Each one of them, a unique blend of skill, determination, and a touch of reckless abandon, craved the taste of victory.

There was
Jackson "The Outlaw" Carter
, a name
whispered with a mixture of awe and fear. He was the reigning champion, a legend carved in the dirt of this track.
His reputation preceded him, a whirlwind of speed and aggression. He lived for the adrenaline rush, the roar of the crowd, and the feeling of pushing his car, and himself, to the limit. Behind that steely gaze, there was a hunger

that burned hotter than the engine of his car.

Then there was
Samantha "The Siren" Evans
, the lone female in this testosterone-fueled world. She was a force to be reckoned with, her driving as smooth and elegant as a ballet, yet as fierce and precise as a predator. With an air of quiet confidence, she navigated the treacherous turns, a calculated risk-taker who never backed down from a

challenge. They said she was cursed by her own ambition, the thirst for victory driving her further than any other.

There was **Mark "The Machine" Johnson**, a quiet giant with a mechanical mind. He built his cars with precision and dedication, a meticulous engineer who saw beauty in the complexities of engines and gears. On the track, he was a cold, calculating strategist, his every move calculated, his every corner precise. He lacked the flamboyant showmanship of others, but his dedication to perfection spoke volumes.

Then there was **Lucas "The Rookie" Hayes**, a fresh face in this world, his youthful exuberance masked by a nervous tension. He was a wildcard, a raw talent with raw ambition. He was hungry to prove himself, driven by a burning desire to escape the shadow of his father, a legend in the racing world who had met a tragic end on this very track.

There was **William "The Fox" Taylor**, a cunning strategist, a master of deception. He was the master of mind games, a player who played the game as a game, his mind always a step ahead of the competition. He was always watching, always analyzing, a predator lurking in the shadows, waiting for the opportune moment to strike.

And there was **Ellie "The Mechanic" Rodriguez**, a woman who commanded respect even in the testosterone-charged pit crews. With grease on her hands and a fire in her eyes, she was the soul of the team, the one who kept the cars running, the one who kept the team together. She was a whisper in the wind, a ghost in the shadows, often overlooked, but never underestimated.

These were the devils of dirt track racing, each with their own demons, their own motivations, their own stories to tell.

The track was their battlefield, the checkered flag their ultimate prize. They were warriors, gladiators in a high-speed ballet, fueled by a lust for victory, their ambition driving them to the edge, to the brink of their own destruction.

Beyond the bright lights and the roaring engines, there was a world of secrets and shadows, a world where the line
between right and wrong blurred with every turn. This was a world where loyalty was tested, where alliances were forged and broken, where betrayal became a currency of survival.

Under the flashing lights, the pressure mounted, a constant hum that vibrated in the air, a reminder of the high stakes involved. These were not just drivers, they were individuals, each with a story, a past, a present, and a future they were fighting for. Every turn of the wheel, every push of the pedal, every drop of sweat, was a testament to their
unwavering ambition, their burning desire for victory.

This was not just a race, this was a fight for survival, a battle for glory, a dance with destiny. The engines roared, the wheels spun, and the devils of dirt track racing were ready to unleash their fury upon the world.

A GLIMPSE BEHIND THE CURTAIN

The pit lane was a symphony of chaos, a whirlwind of activity that mirrored the tempestuous energy coursing through the veins of the drivers and crew members. The air buzzed with the electric anticipation of the upcoming race, a palpable tension that hung heavy in the humid summer air.
Beneath the fluorescent glare of the pit lights, men and women moved with a practiced efficiency, their movements synchronized with the rhythmic hum of wrenches and the hiss of compressed air.

The drivers, clad in fire-resistant suits, stood on the edge of the pit boxes, their eyes fixed on their cars, their minds already locked in a strategic dance. Each driver, a chess piece in this high-stakes game, knew that every maneuver, every decision, would influence the unfolding battle on the track. The atmosphere crackled with a potent mixture of camaraderie and competition, a volatile cocktail that could quickly turn deadly.

"Engine sounds good, boss," said Jake, the chief mechanic, his voice barely audible over the roar of a nearby engine being revved. He wiped the sweat from his brow, his face etched with a blend of determination and fatigue. He'd been working on these cars for years, pouring his heart and soul into each machine, knowing that their performance was inextricably linked to his own reputation.

"Just make sure she's got that extra edge," replied Mark, the driver, his voice gruff, his gaze unwavering. He was a seasoned veteran of the dirt track scene, his years of experience honed into an unyielding instinct for speed. His eyes held a fire that burned brighter than the track lights, fueled by a relentless hunger for victory.

Jake nodded, understanding the unspoken demand in Mark's voice. There was a silent code amongst the drivers and crew members, an understanding that pushed them beyond their limits. It was a code forged in the crucible of competition, fueled by a desire to outdo each other, to conquer the track and claim their share of the glory.

Standing a few feet away, their faces illuminated by the flickering glow of the pit lights, were the rival crew. The members of the opposing team were a stark contrast to Mark and Jake. Their faces were etched with a cold professionalism, their movements calculated and efficient. The tension between the two teams was palpable, a silent war fought in the shadows of the pit lane.

The driver, a young and brash newcomer named Ryan, radiated an aura of cocky confidence, his eyes reflecting an almost desperate hunger for success. He had the talent, the drive, and the unwavering belief that he could surpass even the most seasoned veterans. But beneath that swagger, a gnawing doubt lurked, a fear of failure that fueled his ambition. He needed to prove himself, not only to the racing world but also to his father, a legendary driver who had vanished from the scene under a cloud of controversy.

The pit crew, led by Ryan's father's old nemesis, a wizened veteran named Rusty, mirrored their driver's intensity. They were a team of grizzled veterans, seasoned by years of racing under the harsh glare of the dirt track spotlight. They were masters of their craft, their hands moving with a precision honed by countless hours spent in the trenches. But beneath the surface, there was a simmering resentment, a lingering animosity towards the son of their former rival.

As the minutes ticked by, the tension in the pit lane grew thicker, an unspoken threat hanging in the air. Each glance, each muttered word, carried the weight of a simmering rivalry. The roar of engines echoed through the air,
amplifying the palpable energy that pulsed between the two teams.

The pit lane was more than just a staging ground for the racers; it was a battleground where the drama unfolded, where the rivalries were born and nurtured, where the seeds of deceit and betrayal were sown.

The pit crew members, often overlooked in the glamour of the racing world, were the unsung heroes, the silent partners who toiled tirelessly behind the scenes. They were the ones who held the fate of the drivers in their hands, their skill and expertise determining the outcome of the race. They were the ones who saw the drivers at their most vulnerable,
witnessing the highs and lows of their lives, the sacrifices they made in pursuit of their dreams.

"Mark, your car is ready," Jake announced, his voice filled with a quiet pride. He had poured his heart and soul into this machine, meticulously tuning and refining every component until it hummed with a power that could only be unleashed on the track.

Mark nodded, his eyes gleaming with the glint of a predator about to hunt. He was ready. He stepped into the cockpit, the familiar scent of leather and gasoline filling his senses.

The starter's signal was imminent, and the pit lane was abuzz with a final flurry of activity. The drivers, each with a story to tell, a past to overcome, and a future to shape, were poised to unleash the fury of their engines.

The crowd roared, their cheers echoing through the air. The race was about to begin.

THE FIRST CLASH

The air crackled with anticipation, a symphony of roaring engines and the excited chatter of thousands. The smell of burnt rubber and gasoline hung heavy in the air, a potent cocktail that intoxicated the senses. The track, a dirt oval bathed in the golden light of the setting sun, was a stage for a high-stakes drama about to unfold. This was no ordinary race; this was dirt track Late Model racing, where the roar of engines masked a hidden world of ambition, betrayal, and relentless pursuit of glory.

At the heart of this world were two men, driven by a shared passion for the sport and an insatiable thirst for victory. Jake "The Snake" Taylor, a seasoned veteran with a reputation for ruthless tactics and a string of championship wins to his name, was a legend on the track. His confidence was almost unnerving, his eyes holding a steely glint that reflected his unwavering determination. His victory wasn't just about crossing the finish line first; it was about crushing the competition, leaving them in his dust, proving his dominance.

Across the pit lane, a new force had emerged, a young upstart named Ethan "The Flash" Carter. Ethan, a rookie with raw talent and lightning-fast reflexes, was a breath of fresh air in the stagnant world of dirt track racing. His passion for the sport burned with an untamed fire, and his determination was as palpable as the exhaust fumes that billowed from his car. Ethan wasn't content with just winning; he craved the respect of the veterans, the acknowledgment of his skill. He wanted to prove that he wasn't just a flash in the pan, but a force to be reckoned with.

Their rivalry was palpable, a simmering tension that hung in the air like a storm cloud. It wasn't just about winning or losing; it was about proving who was the better driver, who was the true king of the track. Their eyes met across the pit lane, a silent acknowledgment of the battle to come. Jake, with his seasoned smirk, seemed to see Ethan as a challenge, a new obstacle to overcome. Ethan, eyes burning with an unwavering intensity, saw Jake as the ultimate test, the
benchmark against which he measured his own potential.

The first race of the season was a showdown, a test of skill and mettle that set the stage for a season of fierce
competition. The crowd, fueled by anticipation and adrenaline, roared as the green flag dropped, signaling the start of the race. The cars, propelled by powerful engines, shot off the line, a blur of color and noise that engulfed the track. The tension was thick, palpable in the air, as the drivers battled for position, pushing their cars and
themselves to the limit.

Jake, true to his name, weaved through the pack like a snake, using his experience and cunning to gain an advantage. Ethan, with a youthful bravado, held his own, his car a blur of speed and precision as he chased after the veteran. The crowd erupted with each maneuver, each overtake, as the two drivers engaged in a tense, thrilling dance on the track.

The race was a whirlwind of action and strategy, each driver pushing the boundaries of their skills, testing the limits of their cars and their own courage. Jake, with his years of experience, seemed to anticipate every move, countering Ethan's aggression with calculated precision. Ethan, though less experienced, had an uncanny ability to read the track, predicting his opponents' moves and responding with
lightning-fast reflexes.

But it wasn't just about the race itself; it was about the battle of wills between Jake and Ethan. Each maneuver, each near collision, each aggressive overtake was a statement, a challenge to the other's dominance. It was a battle that went beyond the track, extending into the garages and the back alleys, a silent, unspoken war for supremacy.

As the laps ticked down, the tension escalated, the crowd on the edge of their seats, the anticipation palpable. Jake, with a calculated move, made a decisive pass for the lead, his car a blur of power and finesse. Ethan, determined to reclaim his position, pushed his car to its absolute limit, the roar of the engine echoing across the track. The two drivers, locked in a fierce duel, were neck and neck, the finish line a mere whisper away.

In the final moments of the race, a sudden shift in momentum. Ethan, with a daring maneuver, managed to sneak past Jake, taking the lead just before the checkered flag. The crowd erupted, a wave of cheers and excitement as Ethan crossed the finish line first, claiming a surprise victory. Jake, with a scowl on his face, was forced to settle for second place.

The tension between the two drivers was palpable, a storm brewing in the silence. Ethan, adrenaline pumping, stood tall, his victory a testament to his raw talent and unwavering determination. Jake, his eyes narrowed in a steely gaze, took the defeat with a chilling calmness, his silence speaking volumes. The first clash of the season was over, but the battle had only just begun.

The victory was bittersweet. Ethan had proven himself, proving that he wasn't just a flash in the pan, but a force to be reckoned with. But Jake, a veteran of countless battles, wasn't going to let a rookie steal his crown. He saw Ethan as

a threat, a rising star that needed to be extinguished. The rivalry, fueled by ambition and the relentless pursuit of victory, had only just begun, and the dirt track would
become a stage for a clash of titans, a battle that would leave no one unscathed.

The season was young, the race for the championship long and arduous, and the stakes were higher than ever. The world of dirt track Late Model racing was a world of grit, passion, and danger, a world where the line between ambition and desperation blurred, and the pursuit of glory could lead to devastating consequences. For Jake and Ethan, the season was a chance to prove themselves, to claim victory, and to leave their mark on the sport. But it was also a battle for their own survival, a fight against the dark underbelly of a world that would test their limits and challenge their morals.

The first clash was a mere prelude to a season that would forever alter the course of their lives.

SECRETS IN THE SHADOWS

The roar of the engines was a symphony of raw power, a cacophony of sound that resonated through the very bones of the grandstands. The air hung thick with anticipation, a palpable tension that crackled like static electricity as the Late Model racers lined up on the starting grid, their brightly colored cars a blur of movement against the fading twilight.
It was a scene that was both exhilarating and unnerving, a microcosm of the world that existed within the confines of the dirt track.

This was a place where ambition burned hotter than the engines, and where the pursuit of victory was a relentless, all-consuming force. Here, within the confines of the track, the masks came off, revealing the raw, unfiltered desires of the men and women who dared to push their limits and defy the odds.

Among them was Jack "The Hammer" Riley, a seasoned veteran whose reputation preceded him. Jack was a force to be reckoned with, a man whose steely gaze hid a complex web of emotions. His past was a tapestry woven with threads of both triumph and tragedy, and his unwavering
determination masked a deep-seated yearning for redemption.

Standing beside him was his crew chief, "Big" Pete, a grizzled veteran who had witnessed the ebb and flow of the sport for decades. Pete knew the secrets of the track, the nuances of the cars, and the whispers of the drivers that circulated behind closed doors. Pete was a man of few words but his loyalty to Jack was unwavering, an unwavering faith in a man who had been through the fire and emerged, scarred but defiant.

There was also Amelia "The Raven" Carter, a rising star whose relentless drive and fierce determination defied expectations. Amelia was a newcomer to the world of dirt track racing, but her talent was undeniable. Her past was shrouded in mystery, her motivations a puzzle waiting to be unraveled.

But Amelia wasn't the only one with secrets. Behind the polished smiles and carefully crafted facades, each driver harbored their own demons, their own hidden agendas.

The tension in the pit lane was palpable as the drivers prepared for the race. Mechanics hustled about, making last-minute adjustments, their movements synchronized with the urgency of the moment. The smell of gasoline, a familiar scent that spoke of both excitement and danger, hung heavy in the air.

"Jack, you ready for this?" Pete asked, his voice gruff but laced with concern.

"As I'll ever be, Pete," Jack replied, his gaze fixed on the starting grid. "Just tell me how long until they drop the green flag."

The air vibrated with the rumble of the engines, each roar a testament to the power and the sheer audacity of the drivers who dared to push their limits. The starting lights flickered, the countdown began, and the anticipation reached a fever pitch. The roar of the crowd intensified as the green flag waved, releasing the racers into the fray.

The race was a blur of action, a ballet of skill and daring as drivers battled for position. Jack, true to his nickname, unleashed the full fury of his car, weaving through the pack with relentless determination. Amelia, undeterred by the seasoned veterans, held her own, her car a sleek black silhouette against the dirt track.

But the race was about more than just winning. It was about survival, about pushing the boundaries of what was possible, and about the undeniable thrill of the chase. Each turn, each maneuver, was a gamble, a test of will and skill, a dance with fate.

As the race heated up, so too did the tensions between the drivers.

Jack, with his eyes on the checkered flag, engaged in a fierce duel with "Hurricane" Harry, a brash young driver whose talent was matched only by his recklessness. Jack was
determined to assert his dominance, to prove that he was still the king of the track, but Harry was a wildcard,
unpredictable and fearless.

Meanwhile, Amelia found herself caught in a web of intrigue as she encountered a mysterious figure who seemed to know more about her past than she did. The whispers of the racing world, the secrets that circulated behind closed doors, were beginning to unravel, revealing a hidden world of alliances, betrayals, and dangerous games.

As the laps ticked by, the race turned into a desperate
struggle for survival. The drivers, pushed to their limits, were no longer simply competing for the checkered flag, but for something far more profound. They were fighting for their reputations, for their dreams, and for their very souls.

And as the final lap loomed, the air crackled with the anticipation of a shocking climax. The finish line was a mere blink away, but the true race, the battle for dominance that had been brewing beneath the surface, had only just begun.

The roar of the crowd, the smell of burning rubber, the thrill of the chase, and the sense of impending doom – it was a heady cocktail that held the drivers and the spectators captive.

The race had just begun, and the secrets hidden within the shadows were about to spill into the light. The world of dirt track racing, a world where the line between victory and disaster was razor-thin, was about to be turned upside down.

PUSHING LIMITS

The air hung heavy with the scent of gasoline and burnt rubber as the engines roared to life, a symphony of mechanical fury that resonated through the packed grandstands. The dirt track, a brutal canvas of red clay and unforgiving turns, was a battlefield for the drivers who dared to tame its unforgiving nature. Tonight was no ordinary race; it was the championship showdown, a battle for glory and the coveted title of "Late Model King."

Among the contenders were two names that echoed throughout the pit lane: "The Phantom," a young, fearless driver known for his audacious maneuvers and knack for pushing the limits, and "The Veteran," a grizzled veteran whose years of experience and unwavering determination were a formidable combination. The Phantom, whose real name was Jake Carter, was a rising star, fueled by an
insatiable hunger for victory and a rebellious streak that often led him to trouble. The Veteran, nicknamed "Iron Mike," was a legend on the track, a man who had seen it all, won it all, and whose weathered face bore the scars of countless battles.

The starting grid was set, and the drivers, their faces etched with a mixture of anticipation and adrenaline, waited for the green flag to drop. The tension was palpable, a silent roar that pulsed through the crowd as the countdown began.

"Three... two... one... GO!"

The engines erupted in a deafening cacophony, tires spitting gravel as the cars surged forward, a kaleidoscope of paint and horsepower hurtling towards the first turn. The air was thick with smoke and the smell of burning rubber, the track a blur of dust and tire tracks. Jake, in his sleek black car adorned with the Phantom logo, was on the attack, his car slicing through the pack with a precision that spoke of years of practice and an innate understanding of the track's nuances.

Iron Mike, in his weathered red car, remained a steady presence at the front, his experience and calculated moves allowing him to hold his position. But Jake, ever the aggressor, was relentless. He stalked Mike, his car inches from his rear bumper, waiting for the perfect opportunity to strike. The crowd roared with every pass, every near-miss, every inch gained or lost.

The race was a symphony of skill and daring, a testament to the drivers' courage and the unpredictable nature of the track. Each turn was a test of nerve, each bump a potential disaster waiting to happen. Jake, fueled by the thrill of the chase, pushed his car to its limits, his driving bordering on reckless but his instincts were sharp, his reflexes honed to perfection.

Mike, meanwhile, stayed composed, his years of experience allowing him to anticipate Jake's every move. He wasn't afraid to play dirty when necessary, bumping Jake in the turns, using every trick in the book to maintain his lead. The rivalry between the two drivers was intense, a clash of styles that captivated the audience.

The race stretched on, lap after lap, the tension mounting with each passing moment. The sun began to dip below the horizon, casting long shadows across the track, a chilling reminder that the night was closing in. The crowd was on its feet, their voices a deafening roar, their eyes glued to the track as the two drivers battled for the final stretch.

Jake, feeling the heat of the finish line, took a calculated risk. He dove inside Mike, his car a blur of motion as he attempted a daring pass on the inside. But Mike, anticipating the move, slammed on the brakes, forcing Jake to swerve to avoid a collision. The move was risky, bordering on
dangerous, but it bought Mike precious time.

As they crossed the finish line, the crowd erupted. Jake, narrowly edging out Mike, was declared the winner. The victory was bittersweet for Jake, knowing that his victory had come at a high cost. He had pushed the limits, crossed lines, and walked the tightrope between victory and disaster.
As the applause subsided, Jake knew this was just the beginning. He had tasted victory, but the hunger for more was already gnawing at him, a hunger that could lead him down a dangerous path.

Back in the pit lane, Mike, his face etched with a mixture of frustration and grudging respect, watched Jake celebrate. He knew he had been outplayed, outmaneuvered, but he also knew that Jake's victory had come at a steep price. He had seen that reckless streak in Jake before, the hunger that could consume a man, the hunger that led him to make desperate, dangerous choices. Mike knew that Jake had crossed a line, and he wasn't sure if Jake would be able to walk back from it.

The celebration was in full swing, but underneath the cheers and the flashing lights, there was an undercurrent of unease. The air was thick with the smell of victory, but also with the scent of something more sinister, a sense of foreboding that hung in the air like a dark cloud. The race was over, but the real battles had only just begun.

TANGLED WEBS

The air hung thick with the smell of burnt rubber and diesel, a potent cocktail that clung to the worn-out jeans and sweat-soaked t-shirts of the crowd. The roar of engines was a primal symphony, an insistent pulse that resonated through the weathered stands and reverberated in the chests of those who gathered. This wasn't just a race; it was a spectacle, a ritual, a battle for dominance played out on the unforgiving surface of the dirt track. The stakes were high, the
competition fierce, and the drivers, each with their own intricate web of ambition and desire, were ready to risk everything for the thrill of the checkered flag.

In the heart of this gladiatorial arena, amidst the chaos and adrenaline, a complex dance of alliances and betrayals was unfolding. The drivers, like pawns in a grand game, were maneuvering, shifting, and colliding, their motives as
intricate as the intricate patterns of the checkered flag. Each driver, with their unique blend of skills and personalities, was playing their part, but beneath the surface of the
competitive facade, there were shadows of ambition and deceit.

Ethan "The Outlaw" Carter, the reigning champion and a driver with a reputation for reckless abandon and a penchant for pushing boundaries, had a reputation for winning, but also for pushing the limits, both on and

off the track. His fierce determination and unwavering confidence made him a force to be reckoned with, but it also made him a magnet for envy and resentment. There were whispers of his
ruthlessness, tales of daring moves on the track and underhanded tactics in the pits.

Then there was Riley "The Rook" Jackson, the young, up-and-coming driver with a raw talent and a hunger for victory.
His rise to prominence was meteoric, his raw talent and unwavering dedication quickly earning him the respect of both fans and rivals. Riley was the newcomer, the one who saw everything with fresh eyes, unburdened by the weight of past triumphs and the ghosts of past mistakes. He carried a youthful naiveté, a belief in the inherent fairness of the
game, a belief that Ethan was quick to exploit.

Their rivalry was a simmering cauldron, a constant tension that crackled beneath the surface of every race. They were polar opposites in their approach to the sport, but their paths were inextricably linked. Ethan, the seasoned veteran, saw Riley as a threat to his dominance, a rising tide that
threatened to wash away his legacy. Riley, on the other hand, saw Ethan as a challenge, a benchmark to be surpassed.
Their clashes on the track were legendary, battles of wills fought with the ferocity of gladiators. But their rivalry was far more than a mere competition for the checkered flag; it was a clash of philosophies, a battle of ambition and desire.

Their rivalry was not confined to the racetrack. The drama spilled over into the pit lanes and the dimly lit bars that were the after-race haunts of the racing community. It was a game of whispered promises, veiled threats, and strategic alliances.
Ethan, with his years of experience and a network of
contacts that stretched across the racing world, was a master of manipulation, a player who knew how to move the pieces to his advantage. Riley, with his innocence and a heart that was still untainted by the harsh realities of the sport, was a target for Ethan's scheming.

Ethan, with his cunning and his intimate knowledge of the inner workings of the sport, knew how to use the media to his advantage. He orchestrated events, staged confrontations, and spun narratives to create a public persona that was both menacing and magnetic. The media, hungry for drama and controversy, lapped it up, fueling the rivalry and amplifying Ethan's position as the villain. Riley, with his good looks, his youthful charm, and his raw talent, became the media darling, the underdog hero, the one who stood to challenge the reigning king.

The rivalry had its victims. Ethan, with his ruthless pursuit of victory, had a string of broken promises and shattered alliances. He had left behind a trail of bitter rivals and broken hearts. Riley, with his naiveté and his trust in the system, was vulnerable to exploitation. He was used, manipulated, and ultimately betrayed by those he thought were his allies.

The game of alliances and betrayals extended beyond the immediate rivalry. The owners of the teams, the sponsors, the mechanics, and even the families of the drivers, all played their roles in this intricate dance of power and influence. There were whispers of secret deals, of shady arrangements, of fortunes made and fortunes lost, all in the pursuit of the ultimate prize, the checkered flag.

Amidst this whirlwind of ambition and deceit, love was an unexpected element. Ethan, despite his reputation as a ruthless competitor, had a soft spot, a vulnerable side. He was drawn to Sarah, a fiery young woman who saw beyond the facade of the "Outlaw" and saw the man beneath the persona. Their relationship was a clash of personalities, a dance of opposites, a whirlwind of passion and chaos.

Their relationship was a dangerous game, a delicate balance of love and ambition. Ethan, driven by his desire to win, was constantly pushing the boundaries, testing the limits of Sarah's loyalty and understanding. Sarah, caught between her love for Ethan and her desire for a stable and honest life, was forced to make difficult choices.

Riley, with his innocence and his unwavering belief in good, was drawn to Emily, a young woman who worked as a mechanic in the pit lane. Their connection was grounded in shared dreams and aspirations. They were two souls who were drawn together by a shared passion for the sport and a yearning for something more.

The racing world, with its blend of adrenaline, ambition, and deceit, was a breeding ground for love and betrayal. The players, with their complex relationships and intertwined destinies, were navigating a treacherous landscape of passion and power. Their lives were a whirlwind of emotions, a delicate dance between love and ambition, loyalty and
betrayal. The race was more than a competition for the
checkered flag; it was a game of hearts, a battle for love and dominance, a story of passion and power, played out on the unforgiving stage of the dirt track.

As the cars roared through the turns, the dust swirling in a cloud of chaos, the players in this game of love and ambition were locked in their own personal battles. The checkered flag, the symbol of victory and the culmination of all their efforts, was a distant, yet tantalizing, goal. But the real
victory, the ultimate prize, lay in the tangled web of
relationships that they had woven, the love they had found, and the sacrifices they had made, both on and off the track.
In the end, it was not just the checkered flag that mattered, but the journey, the twists and turns, the highs and lows that had shaped their lives and their destinies.

LOVE AND DECEPTION

The roar of the crowd was deafening, a wave of sound that washed over the infield and vibrated through the grandstands. The air crackled with anticipation, the smell of burnt rubber and gasoline thick in the air. Under the bright lights of the dirt track, the cars were a blur of color and motion, their engines screaming in a symphony of
mechanical fury.

> This was the world of dirt track Late Model racing, a world where the stakes were high, and the competition was fierce.

In this arena of horsepower and grit, drivers pushed their machines and themselves to the limit, chasing the elusive thrill of victory.

Among them was Riley Hayes, a young driver with a burning desire to prove himself. His ambition was as vast as the night sky above the racetrack, his eyes focused on the checkered flag that marked the ultimate triumph. Riley was a rising star in the dirt track scene, known for his daring
maneuvers and relentless determination. He was a charismatic figure, a natural-born competitor, with a smile that could charm anyone, even his fiercest rivals.

But beneath his confident exterior, Riley carried a secret that weighed heavily on his heart. It was a secret that connected him to the enigmatic figure of Ava Pierce, a woman whose beauty and mystery captivated him.

Ava wasn't your typical racing queen. She wasn't caught up in the glamour and the glitz of the racing world. Ava
preferred to stay in the shadows, working behind the scenes as the manager of a prominent racing team. Her sharp mind

and strategic thinking were a formidable force in the competitive landscape of dirt track racing.

Riley and Ava's paths had crossed under the vibrant lights of the racetrack, their initial encounter a fleeting glimpse
amidst the chaotic energy of the sport. A shared glance, a spark of recognition, a subtle touch that lingered long after they parted ways.

Their connection grew in the shadows, whispered secrets shared in clandestine meetings, their stolen moments a fragile flame flickering against the backdrop of the high-stakes world they inhabited.

Their love, however, was built on a foundation of deceit, a secret that threatened to unravel the delicate web of their lives. Ava was a master manipulator, skilled at playing the game, and Riley, blinded by his passion, was caught in her web of intrigue.

Ava's true motives remained shrouded in mystery, her intentions as elusive as the wind that swept across the racetrack. She used her influence, her charm, and her intelligence to navigate the treacherous waters of the racing world, pulling strings from behind the scenes. Her power extended beyond the racing circuit, reaching into the murky depths of the underworld.

Riley, unaware of Ava's true nature, found himself drawn to her like a moth to a flame. He was captivated by her beauty, her intelligence, her enigmatic aura, and her undeniable power. She offered him a glimpse of a world beyond the racetrack, a world of luxury and privilege, a world where the rules were bent, and the stakes were higher than ever before.

But as their romance blossomed, so did the risks. The lines between their worlds blurred, and the consequences of their love affair grew increasingly perilous.

One evening, under the soft glow of the setting sun, Riley and Ava shared a stolen moment at a secluded spot overlooking the racetrack.

"I don't know how much longer I can keep this up," Riley confessed, his voice tinged with concern. "The secrets, the lies, it's wearing me down."

Ava leaned closer, her eyes shimmering with a knowing glint. "It's just a game, Riley," she whispered, her fingers gently stroking his cheek. "A game we have to play to win."

"But what if we lose everything?" Riley asked, his voice laced with doubt.

Ava's smile was as cold as the night wind. "We won't lose, Riley. I won't let us lose. Trust me."

But Riley's trust in Ava was starting to waver. He felt a growing unease, a nagging sense that something wasn't quite right.

Ava was skilled at concealing her true intentions, masking her manipulative tactics with a façade of love and affection. Riley, blinded by his passion, was oblivious to the danger lurking beneath the surface. He clung to the hope that their love was genuine, that Ava's motives were pure.

He couldn't shake the feeling that something was off, that Ava was hiding something from him. Her words, her actions, the secrets she kept, they all pointed towards a darker truth that he couldn't quite grasp.

He couldn't deny the truth that Ava was involved in something much bigger than just the racing world. Her connections, her power, her influence, they all hinted at a world of shadowy deals, hidden agendas, and dangerous secrets.

The more time he spent with Ava, the more he felt caught in a tangled web of deception, a game where the rules were constantly changing, and the stakes were higher than he ever imagined.

Their love was a dangerous game, a gamble that could cost them everything.

As the season progressed, the pressure mounted, and Riley's doubts intensified. The secrets that Ava kept weighed heavily on his mind, a constant reminder of the hidden truths that threatened to destroy everything they had built.

One fateful night, at the track, Riley overheard a conversation that shattered his world. It was a chance encounter, a fleeting moment of truth that unveiled the dark reality behind Ava's enigmatic façade.

The revelation was a bitter pill to swallow, a truth that shattered his illusions and left him reeling. Ava was not the woman he thought she was. Her motives were not pure, her intentions were not genuine. She had been playing him from the very beginning, using him to achieve her own sinister goals.

The realization was a harsh wake-up call, a sudden jolt of reality that forced Riley to confront the truth. He was caught in a game he didn't understand, a game where the stakes were far higher than he ever imagined.

The weight of betrayal was crushing, leaving him shattered and lost. The love he had felt for Ava, the trust he had placed in her, it all crumbled into dust, leaving behind a bitter taste of disillusionment and pain.

His world was now fractured, his life thrown into chaos. He was left to pick up the pieces, to grapple with the
consequences of his misguided passion, and to face the reality of a love built on lies and deception.

The racetrack, once a symbol of his dreams, now represented a painful reminder of his shattered illusions. The roar of the engines, the smell of burnt rubber, the thrill of the race, it all seemed to mock his pain, a constant reminder of the
dangerous game he had played and the ultimate cost of his misguided love.

THE PRICE OF AMBITION

The roar of the crowd was deafening, a cacophony of cheers, screams, and the thunderous rumble of engines. The air crackled with anticipation, thick with the smell of burnt rubber and gasoline. This was the world of dirt track Late Model racing, a gladiatorial spectacle where the line between passion and obsession blurred, and the pursuit of victory overshadowed everything else.

Ethan Carter, a young driver with a hunger for success that burned hotter than the exhaust fumes spewing from his car, gripped the steering wheel, his knuckles white. This race, the final one of the season, was his last shot at the
championship. He was neck-and-neck with his rival, Marcus "The Hammer" Hayes, a veteran driver with a reputation for ruthlessness that matched his nickname.

The green flag dropped, and the cars surged forward, a blur of paint and chrome tearing across the dirt track. Ethan, his heart pounding in his chest, navigated the twists and turns with precision and daring, the roar of his engine a symphony of power and aggression. He could feel the heat of the other cars bearing down on him, the smell of burning rubber acrid in his nostrils.

But the relentless pursuit of victory was taking its toll. As the race raged on, Ethan found himself pushing his car, and himself, beyond their limits. The air grew thick with tension, the smell of burnt rubber intensified, and the roar of the crowd became a deafening, echoing symphony.

"Ethan, you need to slow down," his crew chief, a grizzled veteran named Jake, warned him over the radio. "You're taking too many risks."

"I'm not going to lose this," Ethan growled, his voice strained. "I'm going to win."

Ethan ignored Jake's warnings, his desire for victory burning hotter than ever. He knew he was on the edge, pushing his car, and himself, to their limits. He could feel the car
straining under the immense pressure, the engine screaming in protest. He was in a desperate race against time, against his rival, against himself.

He caught a glimpse of Marcus Hayes's car in his rearview mirror, the veteran driver's face a mask of grim determination. The two cars were practically nose-to-nose, a dance of steel and fury under the glaring lights of the track.
Ethan's hands tightened on the steering wheel, his pulse a frantic drumbeat against his ribs.

In a moment of reckless abandon, Ethan decided to make a risky move. He took a sharp turn, cutting off a slower car, the roar of the crowd rising to a fever pitch. He knew it was dangerous, a gamble with the highest stakes, but he was willing to do anything to win.

But it was a gamble that came with a price. As Ethan sped out of the turn, he realized he had miscalculated. He had pushed too hard, too fast, and his car was out of control. It spun, tires screeching, the car a projectile of metal and fury hurtling toward the wall.

Time seemed to slow down. Ethan could see the wall looming closer, a terrifying, concrete monolith that threatened to crush him. He could feel the sickening lurch of the car as it slammed into the wall, the impact sending a wave of pain through his body.

Then, there was silence.

Ethan opened his eyes, his vision blurry, his head throbbing. He was still alive, but the car was a mangled wreck, a testament to his reckless ambition. As the crowd roared, a mix of cheers and gasps, Ethan realized he had paid a heavy price for his pursuit of victory. He had escaped death, but his car was totaled, his career hanging by a thread. He had tasted defeat, but it was a bitter pill to swallow, mixed with the lingering fear of what could have been.

As paramedics rushed him to the hospital, Ethan couldn't shake the feeling of guilt. He had crossed a line, pushed himself beyond his limits, and in doing so, he had put his own life, and the lives of others, in danger. He had been consumed by ambition, a force that had driven him to make reckless choices, choices that had ultimately backfired.

The incident became a turning point in Ethan's life. It forced him to confront the dark side of his ambition, the insatiable desire for victory that had blinded him to the consequences of his actions. As he lay in the hospital bed, his body aching, his mind racing, he realized that the price of his ambition had been far higher than he had ever imagined.

His injuries healed, but the scars remained, both physical and psychological. He had to learn to control his ambition, to channel his desire for victory into something more than just a reckless pursuit of the checkered flag. It was a hard lesson, but one that he had to learn if he wanted to survive, not just in racing, but in life.

As he returned to the track, he was a changed man. He was still driven by the same fire, the same burning desire to win, but now he had a newfound respect for the dangers of the

sport, and a deeper understanding of the importance of safety and responsibility.

He knew that the price of ambition was high, and he was determined to ensure that he would never have to pay it again. He would race with the same passion, the same
intensity, but with a newfound sense of caution and self-awareness. He would chase victory, but he would do so with the knowledge that there was more at stake than just the checkered flag.

The world of dirt track Late Model racing was a dangerous one, a crucible that tested not only skill and endurance, but also the limits of human ambition. Ethan had learned a hard lesson, and he was determined to never forget it. He would race with passion, with fire, but also with caution and respect for the dangers that lurked beneath the surface of this high-stakes sport. He would chase victory, but he would do so with the knowledge that the price of ambition could be
devastating, and that it was a price he was no longer willing to pay.

A DANGEROUS PROPOSITION

The air hung heavy with the scent of gasoline and burnt rubber, a familiar olfactory cocktail that clung to the corrugated metal walls of the makeshift garage. Inside, the dim light from a single bare bulb illuminated a scene of organized chaos. The air was thick with tension, a palpable current that vibrated between the men gathered around a dented Late Model race car.

John "Bulldog" Riley, a man built like a bear with a perpetually furrowed brow, surveyed his handiwork. He ran a calloused hand over the worn leather of his racing gloves, his fingers tracing the outlines of the worn-out stitching. The gloves were more than just protective gear, they were a testament to his years on the track, a silent chronicle of victories and defeats.

"She's ready, boys," Bulldog declared, his voice hoarse from shouting instructions and the strain of the long day. His words were met with a chorus of grunts and nods. The crew, a motley bunch of grease-stained and sun-weathered
individuals, each possessed a unique skill set, a necessary ingredient in the high-stakes world of dirt track racing.

Bulldog's eyes met the gaze of his friend and rival, a cunning fox of a man named Jack "The Viper" Thorne. Jack, a man of cunning and calculated moves, his eyes sparkled with a predatory glint, always sizing up the competition, always plotting his next maneuver.

"You sure about this, Bulldog?" Jack asked, his voice low and smooth, a stark contrast to Bulldog's gruff baritone. "This deal's gonna put you in deep, you know that, right?"

Bulldog snorted, a defiant puff of air escaping his nostrils. "Deep ain't nothin' new to me, Viper. Been there, done that.
This ain't about money, it's about winning."

Jack leaned back, a smug grin spreading across his lips. "Winning? Or somethin' else? You're the one who's been talkin' about gettin' out of this game for years. Now, all of a sudden, you're gonna risk it all for a few extra bucks?"

Bulldog narrowed his eyes, his gaze unwavering. "We both know this ain't just about the money, Jack. This is about somethin' bigger, somethin' that goes beyond this track. It's about proving we got what it takes, to be the best, even if it means pushing the boundaries."

Jack's grin widened, a flicker of respect betraying his facade. "You always were a stubborn son of a gun, Bulldog. But you're right, there's somethin' else at stake. This isn't just another race, it's a gamble that could change everything."

The tension in the garage thickened as the men exchanged unspoken truths. They were veterans of a ruthless game, a world where victory was everything, and where morals often took a backseat to ambition. They knew the risks involved in the dangerous proposition that lay before them.

"I've been doin' this for too long," Bulldog said, the weariness in his voice a stark contrast to his bravado. "Too many seasons, too many nights under these lights, too many near-misses. I'm tired of livin' on the edge, of never quite gettin' there. I need somethin' more, somethin' to prove I'm not just another face in the crowd."

Jack nodded, understanding flickering in his eyes. "This

deal, it ain't somethin' you'd normally go for, I know that.

But it's a chance to break out, to show 'em who's really got the fire in their belly." He leaned in, his voice dropping to a conspiratorial whisper. "It's a chance to show them the true devils of dirt track racing."

Bulldog's eyes narrowed, the fire of ambition reignited within them. "That's what we're gonna do, Viper," he declared, his voice a guttural growl that echoed through the dusty confines of the garage. "We're gonna show 'em what we're capable of. We're gonna be the ones they talk about long after the checkered flag falls."

The words hung in the air, heavy with the weight of their implications. This wasn't just a race, this was a gamble, a high-stakes proposition that could deliver ultimate victory, but also a devastating fall. They were on the edge, poised on a precipice that promised both glory and destruction. The question was, could they control their destiny, or would the devils of dirt track racing claim them?

THE DEAL

The proposal had been whispered to Bulldog a few days before, a proposition shrouded in secrecy and veiled promises. The man who had made the offer, a shadowy figure known only as "The Fixer," had been a recurring presence in the shadows of the racing world, a whisper of intrigue and potential opportunities. The Fixer's reputation preceded him, a mixture of respect and fear. He was said to have connections that reached deep into the underbelly of the racing circuit, a man capable of manipulating the system in his favor.

The deal was simple: Bulldog, with his fierce competitive spirit and years of experience, was to win the upcoming Grand Prix. The prize, a substantial sum of money that could secure Bulldog's financial future, was tempting. The catch, however, was a clandestine agreement, an unspoken pact that could leave him forever tainted.

"It's gonna be a tight race," The Fixer had said, his voice raspy and low, his eyes gleaming with an unsettling intensity.
"But with the right support, you'll be able to take the checkered flag."

The right support, as The Fixer explained, meant a subtle influence, a nudge in the right direction, a way to ensure Bulldog's victory. It was a risky proposition, a dangerous game that could propel him to unprecedented heights, but could also drag him down into the depths of corruption.

The Fixer had been careful to leave the specifics of the "support" vague, leaving Bulldog to interpret it in his own way. Bulldog had been tempted, the lure of the prize too strong to resist. But he had hesitated, his conscience fighting with his ambition.

"This is a whole new level of play, Bulldog," Jack had said, his voice a mixture of excitement and caution. "This ain't just about winnin' on the track, it's about winnin' the game, about playin' by a different set of rules."

Jack's words had resonated with Bulldog. He knew it was a gamble, a high-stakes proposition that could redefine his career, that could make him a legend. But it also carried the potential for ruin, for his reputation to be shattered, for his world to crumble around him.

THE WEIGHT OF THE DECISION

IN THE DIMLY LIT GARAGE, AS THE HUM OF TOOLS AND THE SCENT OF ENGINE OIL FILLED THE AIR, BULLDOG WRESTLED WITH THE WEIGHT OF his decision. He had spent his life on the track, his entire existence defined by the roar of engines and the thrill of competition. Now, the opportunity to achieve ultimate success, to reach the pinnacle of his sport, lay before him, tantalizingly close, yet shrouded in a dangerous ambiguity.

The money, of course, was a significant factor. It was a chance to escape the financial struggles that had plagued him for years, to provide for his family, to finally feel secure. But it wasn't the only driving force. There was something else, a fire that burned deep within him, a thirst to be the best, to prove himself not only to the racing world, but to himself.

He had always been a man of honor, a driver who raced with integrity, who took pride in his achievements. The proposition, however, forced him to question his values, to consider crossing the line, to embrace a darkness that he had always avoided.

The thought of betraying his principles, of playing the dirty game that the Fixer demanded, gnawed at him. It was a dangerous path, a path that could lead to the destruction of everything he had worked for. But the temptation was overwhelming, the allure of victory too strong to ignore.

He looked at his crew, his loyal band of brothers who had shared his triumphs and failures, who had stood by him through thick and thin. Their faces were etched with years of hard work and dedication, their eyes reflected the shared passion for the sport. He could see the trust they had in him, the faith they placed in his leadership.

Bulldog's chest tightened, the weight of their trust bearing down on him. He knew that betraying their faith, that crossing the line for personal gain, would be an unforgivable act.

His gaze met Jack's, a silent exchange of unspoken truths. Jack knew the risks, he understood the consequences, but he also understood the power that lay within this proposition. He was a man of ambition, a man who thrived in the high-stakes world of dirt track racing, a man who saw the
potential for greatness in this risky deal.

"You're the one who's gotta decide, Bulldog," Jack said, his voice soft but firm. "It's your call, your life, your career. But remember, this ain't just a race, this is a chance to rewrite your story. What's it gonna be?"

The decision weighed on Bulldog's shoulders, a burden that threatened to crush him. He was a man of contradictions, a man torn between his principles and his ambition. The devils of dirt track racing whispered in his ear, tempting him with the promise of ultimate victory, but also warning him of the potential for a devastating fall. The fate of his career, the fate of his soul, hung in the balance.

RISING STAKES

The summer heat clung to the asphalt like a second skin, radiating up from the track and baking the grandstands. It was the heart of the season, and the Late Model racing circuit was in full swing. The air buzzed with anticipation, a tangible energy crackling between the tightly packed rows of cars and the roaring engines. It was a world where the smell of burnt rubber and gasoline mingled with the sweet scent of honeysuckle and the distant tang of barbeque smoke. This was where the Devil's of Dirt Track Racing lived.

The championship battle had heated up, fueled by the relentless pursuit of the coveted title and the ever-present threat of crushing defeat. The pressure mounted with each passing race, squeezing every ounce of talent and grit from the drivers. The roar of the engines was a symphony of raw power and unbridled aggression, each car a weapon wielded by a driver possessed by the need to conquer.

Jack "The Hammer" Riley, a seasoned veteran with a steely gaze and a reputation for ruthlessness, felt the weight of expectation bearing down on him. His loyal crew, led by the grizzled mechanic, Big Ed, worked tirelessly, their hands smeared with grease and their faces etched with the grime of the track. Jack had a fierce determination to win, a fire
burning inside him fueled by years of struggle and the taste of victory. He wasn't just racing for a championship;

he was fighting for something more.

But Jack was not alone in his pursuit. His biggest rival, the young and brash Marcus "The Maverick" Jones, had emerged as a formidable challenger. Marcus was a whirlwind of talent and reckless ambition, pushing the limits of both himself and his car. His daring maneuvers and reckless disregard for the rules had earned him both admiration and disdain. He had a devil-may-care attitude that made him unpredictable and terrifyingly dangerous on the track.

The tension between the two drivers was palpable, a silent war waged with every glance and every calculated move. They were mirror images of each other, both driven by a hunger for the top spot, but fueled by vastly different motivations. Jack, weathered by the trials of life, chased redemption, while Marcus, fueled by a thirst for power, chased glory.

The championship contenders were not the only ones feeling the heat. The pressure was also felt by the families, the sponsors, and the crew members who dedicated their lives to the sport. The stakes were higher than ever, with the
potential for both personal and financial ruin looming over the entire circuit.

The rivalry between Jack and Marcus had reached a fever pitch, and their battles on the track had become a spectacle of brute force and calculated aggression. The grandstands erupted with cheers and jeers, fueling the fire of competition. Each race was a battle, a clash of wills and machines where only one could emerge victorious. The tension was thick enough to cut with a knife, the atmosphere charged with anticipation and the threat of disaster.

One particular race, held under the scorching sun of a late summer afternoon, became a defining moment in the season. The track, slick with sweat and a fine layer of dust, was a treacherous labyrinth. The drivers, pushing the limits of their machines and their own endurance, were locked in a deadly dance. The air was thick with the scent of burnt rubber and the acrid smell of desperation.

Jack, in his signature black and red race car, took the lead early on, his experience and precision giving him a slight advantage. Marcus, in his bold blue and silver machine, was not far behind, his aggressive driving style keeping him hot on Jack's tail. The crowd roared as the two cars duelled for the lead, each maneuver a calculated risk, each bump a potential disaster.

The tension ratcheted up with every lap, the roar of the engines a primal scream echoing across the track. The battle for the lead was fierce, a relentless dance between
aggression and strategy. Each driver pushed the boundaries of their cars and their own physical limits, their focus unwavering, their minds locked on the finish line.

The tension wasn't limited to the track. The pit crews,
working with feverish urgency, were under pressure to keep their cars in peak condition. Big Ed, his face etched with worry, and the rest of Jack's team, worked tirelessly, their hands slick with sweat and their minds focused on the task at hand.

The pressure was immense. The possibility of victory was tantalizingly close, yet the threat of disaster was ever-
present. One wrong move, one miscalculation, and the whole season could be thrown into disarray.

As the race reached its final lap, Jack and Marcus were neck and neck. The crowd, on its feet, was a symphony of cheers and shouts. The tension was at a breaking point. The finish line was just a few hundred yards away.

Suddenly, Marcus, in a desperate move, made a daring attempt to pass Jack on the inside. The two cars, a blur of motion, collided with a jarring impact. The crowd gasped as both cars spun out of control.

The air was filled with a cacophony of crunching metal and the screams of the crowd. The race came to a sudden, and unexpected halt. The world seemed to hold its breath.

The tension was palpable, the silence heavy with anticipation. The collision had left both Jack and Marcus shaken but unharmed. Their cars, however, were totaled. The race was over, but the drama was far from finished.

As the dust settled, the aftermath of the collision was a stark reminder of the unpredictable nature of the sport and the high stakes involved. The rivalry had reached its breaking point. The championship was still up for grabs, but the lines between competition and animosity had blurred. The Devils of Dirt Track Racing had shown their true colors, and the pressure had revealed their deepest desires and darkest intentions. The race might be over, but the war had just begun.

CRACKS IN THE ARMOR

The air hung thick with anticipation, a palpable tension that crackled through the crowded grandstands and spilled onto the asphalt of the dirt track. The rumble of engines, a
symphony of raw power and mechanical fury, vibrated through the ground, echoing the pounding hearts of the drivers and the anxious breaths of the spectators. This was the world of Late Model racing, a brutal ballet of speed and aggression where inches separated victory from defeat and where the line between ambition and recklessness blurred into a dangerous haze.

For months, the drivers had been locked in a fierce battle, their hunger for the checkered flag fueled by a potent mix of ego, ambition, and the intoxicating adrenaline rush that pulsed through their veins. But now, with the season winding down, the pressure was mounting, each race a desperate struggle for every point, every inch of ground.

AND WITH THE PRESSURE CAME THE CRACKS.

Jesse "The Maverick" Carter, the reigning champion and the undisputed king of the track, had always been known for his unwavering confidence, his unflinching gaze that seemed to bore into the souls of his rivals. Yet, beneath his cool exterior, doubt was beginning to gnaw at him, a whisper of vulnerability that he fought tooth and nail to suppress. The weight of expectations, the relentless pursuit of perfection, and the shadow of his past failures had begun to take a toll.

The pressure manifested in his driving, pushing him to the edge, forcing him to take risks he would have never considered before. He began to make uncharacteristic mistakes, over-compensating for his perceived weaknesses, leaving him open to attacks from his rivals.

His teammate, the stoic and calculating James "The Shadow" Hayes, had always been the epitome of control, a man whose emotions were as tightly wound as the engine of his car. His calm demeanor was his shield, shielding him from the world's chaos and protecting the secrets he carried. But the relentless heat of the competition, the constant strain of maintaining his composure, and the growing suspicion that his own brother, a rival driver, was playing a dangerous game, began to chip away at his composure.

His eyes, once steely and unreadable, now flickered with a touch of desperation, his hands betraying a tremor that hinted at the turmoil brewing within him. His strategic brilliance, once flawless, now faltered, revealing cracks in the armor of his carefully crafted persona.

The rivalry between the two brothers, James and the volatile, reckless Ethan "The Demon" Hayes, had always been a powder keg, a simmering animosity fueled by years of competition and resentment. But with their father's health failing and the legacy of their family's racing dynasty at stake, the stakes had become even higher, the competition even more fierce.

Ethan, driven by a burning need to prove his worth, to break free from the shadow of his older brother, embraced the darkness within him. He pushed the limits of the sport, pushing the boundaries of acceptable behavior, using ruthless tactics and bending the rules to gain an edge. His driving became a reckless blur, a whirlwind of aggression that left his competitors bruised and his reputation stained.

James, haunted by the fear of losing his father and the family legacy, found himself caught in a difficult position. He knew that Ethan's reckless behavior was dangerous, but he was also hesitant to expose his brother's dark side. The weight of their family's expectations, the pressure to hold the family together, weighed heavily on his shoulders, forcing him to make choices that went against his principles.

Meanwhile, the beautiful and enigmatic Sarah "The Siren" Morgan, the only female driver in the circuit, was struggling with her own demons. She had always been a force to be reckoned with, a skilled driver who defied expectations and demanded respect from her male counterparts. But the relentless sexism, the whispers and doubts, the constant pressure to prove herself had taken their toll.

Her confidence, once unshakeable, had begun to waver. Her focus, once laser-sharp, blurred at the edges, her driving becoming erratic, a reflection of the turmoil within her. She sought solace in the arms of her longtime boyfriend, the charismatic, yet ultimately selfish, Billy "The Showman" Johnson.

Their relationship, once passionate and supportive, had become a tangled web of jealousy, manipulation, and unspoken desires. Billy, fueled by his own ambitions, was willing to sacrifice everything for success, even the woman he claimed to love.

The pressure was mounting, and cracks were appearing everywhere. The relentless pursuit of victory, the constant struggle for survival in this unforgiving world, had begun to take its toll. The masks they wore to protect themselves, the carefully constructed facades that hid their vulnerabilities, were starting to slip, revealing the cracks beneath the surface. Their flaws, their weaknesses, the demons that lurked in the shadows, were beginning to rise to the surface, threatening to shatter the world they had built.

The season was reaching its climax, and the race for the championship was becoming a desperate struggle, a battle for survival where only the strongest would endure. The Devils of Dirt Track Racing were facing their most
formidable opponent: themselves.

The air crackled with anticipation, a palpable tension that hung heavy in the air. The roar of the engines, a symphony of raw power and mechanical fury, vibrated through the grandstands, echoing the pounding hearts of the drivers and the anxious breaths of the spectators. This was the world of Late Model racing, a brutal ballet of speed and aggression where inches separated victory from defeat and where the line between ambition and recklessness blurred into a
dangerous haze.

The final race of the season was upon them, a high-stakes showdown that would determine the champion. The drivers, each carrying the weight of their ambitions and the burden of their past, prepared to take the green flag, their minds a swirling vortex of emotions, their hearts pounding like
drums in their chests.

The air crackled with anticipation, a palpable tension that hung heavy in the air. The roar of the engines, a symphony of raw power and mechanical fury, vibrated through the grandstands, echoing the pounding hearts of the drivers and the anxious breaths of the spectators. This was the world of Late Model racing, a brutal ballet of speed and aggression where inches separated victory from defeat and where the line between ambition and recklessness blurred into a
dangerous haze.

As the green flag waved, the drivers surged forward, their cars a blur of color and motion. The track, a canvas of dirt and dust, was a battleground, each turn a fight for position, each straightaway an opportunity to unleash their power. The air was thick with the smell of burnt rubber and gasoline, the sound of screeching tires and roaring engines a primal symphony.

Jesse Carter, his mind laser-focused, his hands gripping the steering wheel with unwavering determination, pushed his car to the limit. He had to win. He had to prove himself. He had to erase the doubts that haunted him, the whispers of failure that lingered in his mind.

But the pressure was immense, the competition fierce. His rivals, each with their own motives and agendas, were relentless in their pursuit of victory. James Hayes, haunted by his brother's reckless behavior and the weight of his family's legacy, was determined to keep his brother in check, to protect the family name from further disgrace.

Ethan Hayes, fueled by a burning desire to prove himself, to break free from the shadow of his brother, drove with reckless abandon. He took risks, pushed the limits, and left a trail of wreckage in his wake.

Sarah Morgan, battling against the sexism and the doubts that plagued her, fought with a ferocity that defied expectations. She drove with a grace and precision that belied her fragile confidence, but beneath the surface, the pressure was taking its toll.

Billy Johnson, ever the showman, used his charisma and charm to manipulate his opponents, playing them like pawns in a game he was determined to win. He was willing to do whatever it took to achieve his goals, even if it meant sacrificing those around him.

The race was a whirlwind of twists and turns, a chaotic ballet of speed and aggression. The drivers, each pushing their limits, each driven by their own demons, were locked in a desperate struggle for survival. The tension was palpable, the air thick with the scent of danger.

As the laps ticked down, the battle for the championship intensified. Jesse Carter, driven by a desperate need to win, made a daring move, taking a risky pass that nearly ended in disaster. He felt the pressure mounting, his heart pounding in his chest, the weight of his past failures pressing down on him.

James Hayes, watching his brother's reckless driving, made a difficult decision. He had to protect his family, even if it meant sacrificing his own ambitions. He made a strategic move, blocking his brother's path and costing him valuable time.

Ethan Hayes, enraged by his brother's betrayal, lost control of his car, spinning out of control. He was forced to pit for repairs, his hopes for the championship slipping away. His anger simmered, a dangerous heat that threatened to consume him.

The race, a blur of speed and adrenaline, was coming down to the wire. Jesse Carter, his heart pounding in his chest, his mind focused on the finish line, pushed his car to the limit.
He could taste victory, feel the roar of the crowd as he crossed the finish line.

But Sarah Morgan, determined to prove herself, to silence the doubts that had plagued her, made a bold move. She took a daring pass, overtaking Jesse Carter in the final turn, crossing the finish line first.

The crowd erupted in cheers, the noise deafening, a wave of pure excitement washing over the grandstands. Sarah Morgan, her heart pounding in her chest, had done it. She had won.

The world of Late Model racing, a brutal and unforgiving sport, had its first female champion. The Devils of Dirt Track Racing, their masks finally shattered, their vulnerabilities laid bare, had faced their demons and emerged victorious.

The final race of the season had been a crucible, a test of their courage, their resilience, their determination. They had pushed their limits, confronted their demons, and ultimately, they had found redemption. The journey had been arduous, the cost high, but they had survived, emerged stronger, and ready to face whatever challenges lay ahead.

BETRAYAL UNCOVERED

The tension in the air was as thick as the exhaust fumes hanging over the track. It had been building for weeks, simmering beneath the surface of the high-octane world of dirt track racing. Each race was a battle, a test of nerve and skill, but the true battles were being fought in the pits, in the whispered conversations and hidden agendas.

The revelation that had ripped through the tightly knit community like a sonic boom was a betrayal of the most insidious kind. It had been whispered at first, a rumor circulating among the drivers and crew, a shadow cast over the camaraderie that held this world together. But the
whispers quickly hardened into accusations, and the accusations into a bitter truth that poisoned everything.

It started with Danny "The Duke" Dubois, the reigning champion and a force to be reckoned with on the track. He had always been a man of ambition, a driver who pushed the limits of his car and himself to achieve victory. But beneath the confident facade, there was a growing unease. He was always aware of the whispers, the sly glances, the way some avoided his eyes.

The whispers were about his crew chief, Jimmy "The Mechanic" Malone. Jimmy was a legend in the pits, known for his meticulous attention to detail and his unwavering loyalty to Danny. He was more than a crew chief; he was Danny's right hand, his confidante, his brother in arms. But whispers of a hidden deal, a secret pact with a rival team, began to haunt the air.

The rumors reached a fever pitch during a race at the notorious Thunderdome track, known for its unforgiving corners and unforgiving drivers. It was the kind of race where everything was on the line, where every inch counted, and where tempers flared like the sparks of a thousand burning tires.

Danny was leading the pack, his car a blur of speed and power, but something felt off. The car wasn't handling as smoothly as it usually did. The engine sputtered, and the tires screeched as he fought to maintain control. As he rounded a particularly dangerous turn, the car suddenly veered, throwing Danny into a brutal spin.

He slammed into the wall, the impact sending a wave of pain through his body. As the dust settled, Danny stumbled out of the wreckage, his face contorted in a mixture of anger and disbelief. He looked toward the pits, his eyes searching for Jimmy. But Jimmy was nowhere to be seen.

The suspicion gnawed at Danny, a bitter knot of doubt tightening in his stomach. He had trusted Jimmy with his life, his career, his everything. And now, in the face of a catastrophic failure, Jimmy was missing.

Danny was a proud man, a man who had always built his success on grit and talent, but this betrayal felt like a blow to the core of his being. He had been used, manipulated, his trust shattered like the glass of a broken trophy.

The truth emerged in a shocking confrontation. A few days later, as Danny was trying to piece together the wreckage of his car and his dreams, he received a phone call from a voice he hadn't heard in years. It was a voice from his past, a voice that had promised him fame and fortune, a voice that had lured him into this world of high-stakes competition.

The voice belonged to Michael "The Viper" Vance, a notorious figure in the racing world, a driver who had once been Danny's mentor, but who had since become a bitter rival. The Viper was a man who played by his own rules, a man who saw racing as a battlefield where any tactic was fair game. He was a man who thrived on the thrill of the chase, the gamble of the game, and the devastation he left in his wake.

"Danny, my boy," The Viper's voice purred through the phone, laced with a chillingly casual cruelty. "Looks like your little Jimmy boy decided to throw you a curveball, didn't he?"

Danny felt a surge of rage, his fists clenching. "What did you do to him?" he snarled.

"Oh, nothing that wouldn't be perfectly legal," The Viper chuckled. "Let's just say Jimmy's been offered a very compelling opportunity, a chance to take his career to the next level. A chance to work with someone who truly appreciates his talents."

"You bought him off?" Danny's voice was thick with disbelief, tinged with a raw pain that scraped against his pride. "You used him against me?"

"Now, now, Danny," The Viper said, his voice smooth as silk. "Don't be so dramatic. It's just business. Besides, you know the saying, 'all's fair in love and racing.'"

The words were meant to be a taunt, but they hit Danny like a punch to the gut. It was the cold, calculated truth of this world, a truth that had always lurked beneath the surface, but that now stood revealed in all its ugliness.

Danny was forced to confront a harsh reality: he was a pawn in a much larger game, a game where loyalty was a luxury, and betrayal a tool. He had built his entire career on the trust he placed in those around him, but that trust had been shattered, leaving him feeling vulnerable and alone.

As he hung up the phone, Danny knew he had to make a choice. He could let this betrayal consume him, let it cripple his spirit and his resolve. Or he could use it as fuel, a burning desire to prove his worth, to reclaim his place at the top of this brutal, unforgiving world.

The world of dirt track racing had shown him its true colors, and he was determined to fight back. He would expose The Viper's treachery, and he would win, not just for himself, but for the loyalty that had been so carelessly thrown aside.

The air in the garage hung thick with the scent of gasoline and sweat, the hum of machinery a constant background noise. It was a world that demanded dedication, a world that ate you up and spat you out if you weren't strong enough.
Danny was determined to prove he had what it took to survive, to fight back, to become the ultimate survivor in this world of dirt, dust, and deceit.

The betrayal had been a catalyst, a wake-up call that had stripped away the illusions of this world. Now, Danny saw everything for what it truly was: a battlefield where every corner was a potential trap, every handshake a potential betrayal, and every victory a hard-earned triumph. He would use the anger, the hurt, the betrayal to fuel his every move, to push him further, to make him stronger.

Danny was no longer just a driver; he was a warrior. He was a man who had been betrayed, but who had found a new purpose, a new fire in his heart. He would make them pay for what they had done. He would win, not for glory, but for justice.

The next race was just a few weeks away, and Danny was ready. He would drive with a vengeance, his engine roaring with the fury of a wounded beast. The Viper had pushed him to the brink, but Danny was not one to back down. He was about to show them all what a man who had been pushed to his limits could do. He was about to show them the true meaning of "The Devils of Dirt Track Racing."

THE COST OF SECRETS

The whispers started quietly, like the rustle of dry leaves in the wind, a faint rustle at first, then a growing chorus that echoed through the garages and pit stalls, along the winding roads of the dirt track, and finally, into the hearts of the men and women who lived and breathed the lifeblood of dirt track Late Model racing. Secrets, like the dust kicked up by a roaring engine, settled everywhere, coating the world in an unsettling haze.

The whispers began with the hushed confessions of a few, a worried glance exchanged, a hand cupped around a mouth, whispering a name, a deal, a betrayal. They spread through the tight-knit community, infecting the air with suspicion and doubt, turning friends into enemies, and creating a constant undercurrent of tension that permeated every aspect of the season.

The first to crack was the ever-so-confident, fast-talking, and almost too-smooth driver, Johnny "The Jet" Riley. He'd been the heart of the racing scene for as long as anyone could remember, his charisma and speed a winning combination that had made him a local legend. But the Jet's relentless pursuit of victory had a dark side, a side that began to show in the hollowed look in his eyes and the nervous twitch in his jaw. The whispers started around him, fueling a fire of uncertainty in his heart that he couldn't extinguish.

It all started with a simple bet, a wager made in the heat of the moment, a playful challenge between two rivals. The Jet, never one to back down from a challenge, had agreed to stake his latest, pristine Late Model against a sizable sum of money. But the wager wasn't about the money, it was about bragging rights, about proving he was the best in the region. The whispers, however, painted a different picture. They spoke of a hidden agenda, a calculated move to gain an unfair advantage in the season's final race, a race that would determine who would claim the coveted championship title.

The Jet, a man who believed in his own abilities, his skill, and the power of his machine, had initially dismissed the whispers as mere rumors. He was the Jet, he couldn't be outsmarted, he couldn't be bested. But as the season progressed, the whispers grew louder, the doubt more persistent, and the fear of a possible truth gnawed at him, leaving him unable to focus on the only thing that mattered –the checkered flag.

As the whispers reached the ears of his crew, they began to crack, too. The loyal mechanics who had worked alongside the Jet for years, who had helped him conquer countless tracks and triumphs, were now consumed by doubt. Their trust, forged in the fires of competition, was now smoldering under the weight of whispered secrets.

One of the crew members, a young, quiet man named Sam, was the first to confront the Jet. Sam had been the Jet's right-hand man, his confidante, the one who always knew how to keep the engine purring like a well-oiled beast. He was a man who understood the nuances of the machines, the
language of the roaring engine, and the pulse of the racing world. But Sam's quiet demeanor hid a keen mind and an intuitive understanding of the people around him. He had sensed the change in the Jet, the subtle shift in his demeanor, the air of unease that hung about him like a shroud.

"It's not just the whispers, Jet," Sam said one evening, his voice low and steady as they stood under the harsh glow of the garage lights. "It's the way you've been acting, the way you've been looking at the others." Sam couldn't bring himself to utter the words, the whispers that plagued his mind, but the Jet understood. He knew what Sam was referring to.

The Jet, his shoulders slumped, his eyes reflecting the tired weariness of a man carrying a burden he couldn't bear,
simply nodded. He had been trying to convince himself that the rumors were baseless, that his actions were justified, that his ambition was merely a driving force, a thirst for victory that burned within him. But the truth, like the stench of gasoline and burnt rubber, was inescapable. He had taken a shortcut, a dangerous shortcut that promised a victory, a championship, but at a cost. He had allowed his ambition to cloud his judgment, to lead him down a path that was paved with deceit, a path that threatened to consume him entirely.

Meanwhile, a similar storm of whispers raged around the track's reigning champion, the enigmatic and fiercely
competitive driver, Lily "The Lightning" Carter. Lily was the epitome of grace and grit, a woman who had carved her own path in a male-dominated world, leaving a trail of broken records and stunned competitors in her wake. Her eyes, a piercing blue that reflected the determination in her heart, held a fire that was both intimidating and alluring. Lily was a woman who lived for the thrill of the race, for the rush of adrenaline that coursed through her veins as she pushed her machine to its limits, but her reputation as a woman of
integrity was challenged by the whispers that began to swirl around her.

The whispers were about a secret, a personal secret that threatened to unravel the meticulously crafted facade she had built around herself. It was a secret that had been buried deep within her, a secret that had haunted her dreams and kept her up at night, a secret that had the power to tear down the walls she had built around her heart.

The whispers started with a hesitant question from a close friend, a woman who had witnessed Lily's unwavering strength and unwavering determination. But Lily's usual confident demeanor seemed to waver, her usual sharp wit dulling under the weight of the unspoken, the unspoken fear that the truth would finally surface. The whispers spread like wildfire, fueled by the rumors of a past relationship, a betrayal that had left a permanent scar, a secret that threatened to expose her vulnerability.

Lily, always the stoic warrior, tried to ignore the whispers, to keep them at bay, to focus on the race ahead, on the victory that would silence the voices of doubt. But the whispers had a way of finding their way into the cracks of her armor, chipping away at her confidence, reminding her of the vulnerability that she had so carefully concealed.

The weight of the whispers was a heavy burden, a constant reminder of the fragility of her world, a world built on a foundation of secrets and lies. Lily's reputation was everything, her image, her strength, her unwavering spirit, it was all on the line. The thought of her carefully crafted world collapsing around her was a terrifying prospect, a thought that kept her awake at night, her heart pounding in her chest, her mind racing with a thousand scenarios of how the truth could be revealed.

As the whispers became more insistent, Lily found herself drawn to the one person she thought she could trust, a man who had seen the real her, a man who had embraced her vulnerabilities. This man, Jake "The Shadow" Jones, was the crew chief for Lily's team, a man who had dedicated his life to racing, a man who understood the complex world of dirt track racing better than anyone. Jake was a man who could see through the facade, the carefully constructed image that Lily presented to the world. He saw the strength, the determination, but he also saw the vulnerability beneath the surface. He saw the woman behind the champion, the woman who was burdened by her own secrets.

Lily, desperate for someone to confide in, someone to help her navigate the storm that was brewing around her, confided in Jake. She told him about the secret that haunted her, the past that she had tried to bury, the fear that the truth would be exposed. Jake, a man of few words, listened patiently, his eyes reflecting a mix of understanding and concern. He had seen the toll the whispers had taken on Lily, the way they had chipped away at her confidence, the way they had filled her with a sense of dread.

Jake, a man who lived for the thrill of the race, who understood the risks and the consequences, knew that the truth, once exposed, could be a dangerous weapon. He understood the pressure, the relentless pursuit of perfection that Lily felt, and the fear of losing everything she had worked so hard to achieve.

He told Lily, "The truth, like a loose bolt, will eventually find its way out. It's just a matter of time. It's up to you to decide when and how."

The whispers, like the dust that swirled around the track, threatened to engulf them all, The secrets, like the shadows that stretched across the track at dusk, had the power to reshape their lives, to shatter their carefully crafted worlds. The cost of secrets, the price of hiding the truth, was a heavy burden to bear, a burden that threatened to consume them, leaving them lost and adrift in a world where the only
constant was the roar of the engines and the thrill of the race.

A DESPERATE MOVE

The air hung thick with anticipation, the smell of burnt rubber and gasoline a familiar, intoxicating aroma. It was the final lap of the night's race, the grand finale of the Southern Dirt Track Championship, and the tension was palpable. The roar of the engines was deafening, a symphony of
mechanical fury that vibrated through the stands. But within the cockpit of the No. 13 car, it was a quiet symphony, each click of the gear shifter, each adjustment of the steering wheel, a deliberate, calculated movement. At the wheel, Jaxon Pierce, a young, cocky driver with a burning ambition, felt the pressure mounting. He was in the lead, but the
relentless pressure from his rival, the veteran racer, Mason "The Hammer" Hayes, was a constant threat. Their rivalry was one of the most fierce in the circuit, a clash of generations, of experience versus audacity.

Jaxon, a driver known for his aggressive style, had been leading for most of the race. He had pushed his car to its limits, taking risks that bordered on recklessness. But Mason, a veteran of countless races, was a master of strategy, his every move calculated and deliberate. He knew Jaxon's weaknesses, his tendency to push too hard, to take unnecessary risks. He waited for the right moment, the moment Jaxon would falter.

As the race entered the final lap, the crowd erupted, their cheers echoing through the stadium. The pressure on Jaxon was immense. His heart pounded in his chest, his hands gripped the steering wheel, knuckles turning white. The crowd's roar was a deafening chorus, a constant reminder of the stakes. One mistake, one miscalculation, and it would all be over. He glanced at the rearview mirror, seeing Mason's car, a menacing shadow closing in. His rival was gaining ground, his car a blur of speed and power.

The tension in the car was almost unbearable. Jaxon could feel the sweat dripping down his forehead, his vision blurring slightly. He fought to maintain his focus, his mind racing through the possible scenarios. He had to stay ahead. He had to win. His entire career, his future, depended on this race.

But then, a sudden jolt. The car lurched, the engine sputtering. His heart sank. He'd been running his car too hard, pushing it beyond its limits. It was starting to give way, the pressure building, the engine threatening to blow. The crowd's roar seemed to turn into a mocking echo. The dream of victory was slipping away, the taste of defeat bitter on his tongue.

Desperate, Jaxon took a gamble. He knew it was dangerous, reckless, but it was the only chance he had. He shifted down, flooring the accelerator, pushing the engine even harder, ignoring the warning lights flashing on the dashboard. He was pushing his car to its absolute limit, hoping to stay ahead long enough for the finish line to appear. He could hear the engine screaming, the sound a symphony of protest, a warning of imminent disaster.

Mason, sensing Jaxon's desperation, pressed his advantage. He saw the flickering lights on the No. 13 car, knew Jaxon was in trouble. He pushed harder, his car a blur of speed and power. The crowd's roar intensified, the anticipation palpable. They knew something was about to happen, knew this final lap was going to be a spectacle of drama and destruction.

Jaxon, with gritted teeth, held on. He could feel the engine screaming, the car shuddering. He knew he was pushing it too far, but he had to win. He couldn't let Mason take the championship. He couldn't let all his hard work go to waste.

And then, he saw it. The finish line, a beacon of hope in the darkness. A surge of adrenaline coursed through his veins.
He had to make it. He had to finish. With a final burst of power, he surged forward, the engine screaming in protest. He crossed the finish line, a blur of speed and dust, the roar of the crowd echoing in his ears. He had won. But at what cost?

The victory tasted like ashes in his mouth. He knew he had pushed his car to its limits, and he had no idea how much longer it would last. He had won the race, but the damage he had done to the car, the risks he had taken, were going to have repercussions. He had made a desperate move, a move that had cost him more than just his pride.

As he stepped out of the car, the victory celebration a distant roar, he could see the damage. The engine was smoking, the hood hot to the touch. The car, his car, the instrument of his dreams, was on the verge of collapse. His victory was a hollow one, a triumph built on a foundation of desperation. The applause of the crowd, the cheers of his team, faded into a distant memory. He was left with the cold reality of his situation, the knowledge that he had gambled with his future, and the weight of that decision would linger long after the last echoes of the celebration had faded.

FRACTURED CONNECTIONS

The air hung heavy with tension, a palpable electricity crackling between the drivers and their crews. It wasn't just the heat of the summer sun that made the pit lane feel like a pressure cooker. It was the weight of unspoken truths, the festering wounds of betrayal, and the ever-present shadow of ambition that loomed over everything. The camaraderie that had once held them together, the shared passion for the roar of engines and the thrill of victory, was now fractured,
splintered by the relentless pursuit of personal gain.

The relationship between Jake and Riley, once a tight-knit bond forged in the fires of their shared dreams, had become a volatile cocktail of resentment and suspicion. Jake,
consumed by his own ambition, had allowed his desire for victory to cloud his judgment, leading him to a series of decisions that had eroded Riley's trust. Riley, a man of unwavering loyalty and integrity, had been blindsided by Jake's betrayal, the pain of it cutting deep. Their
conversations, once filled with laughter and shared visions, were now strained, laced with accusations and bitterness.

The whispers of Jake's actions, of his reckless maneuvers and calculated manipulations, had spread through the pit lane like wildfire. Even those who had once been Jake's allies, his closest confidantes, now looked at him with a mixture of disbelief and disgust. The respect he had earned over years of hard work and fierce dedication had been tarnished by his hunger for victory at any cost.

Riley, burdened by the weight of Jake's deceit, struggled to reconcile the man he knew with the shadows that seemed to have overtaken him. He had tried to reason with Jake, to appeal to the friendship they once shared, but his pleas had fallen on deaf ears. Jake, entrenched in his own self-serving pursuits, refused to acknowledge the damage he had inflicted.

The pressure mounted with each passing race, pushing them all to the brink. The stakes had never been higher, and the race for the championship title had transformed into a brutal battleground. The lines between friends and rivals had blurred, and the pursuit of victory had become a desperate, all-consuming obsession. The weight of it all began to take its toll, gnawing at their souls, chipping away at their sanity.

The tension reached a fever pitch during a race at a track notorious for its unforgiving turns and high-speed crashes. The roar of the engines was deafening, a primal scream echoing across the sprawling, packed grandstands. The drivers, their faces grim and determined, pushed their cars to the limit, the roar of engines a relentless assault on their senses.

The crowd, a sea of fervent faces, roared with every daring move, their cheers a deafening chorus of excitement and anticipation. Every corner, every pass, was a gamble, a dance with danger that could end in a fiery wreck or a triumphant victory. The drivers, their adrenaline surging, were caught in a vortex of competition, pushing themselves and their machines to the absolute limit.

Jake, his eyes narrowed with fierce determination, refused to back down from a challenge. He threw caution to the wind, his reckless maneuvers pushing the boundaries of what was possible. He squeezed past Riley in a dangerous, high-speed maneuver that sent a jolt of adrenaline through the crowd. Riley, his jaw clenched, gritted his teeth in frustration. The betrayal he had endured, the broken promises, fueled his determination.

The race, a blur of speed and chaos, reached its climax in a heart-stopping finish. The two cars, neck and neck, crossed the finish line in a dead heat. The crowd erupted in a frenzy of excitement, the tension breaking with a roar of cheers and a storm of applause. The judges, their faces grim with the weight of their responsibility, reviewed the footage,
analyzing every corner, every pass, searching for a winner.

The tension was almost unbearable. The drivers, their bodies spent and their minds drained, stood in the pit lane, waiting for the verdict. Jake, his features tense with anticipation, refused to make eye contact with Riley. He had gambled and won, but at what cost?

The announcer's voice echoed across the track, shattering the silence. "We have a winner! After a thrilling race, Jake
emerges victorious!"

The crowd erupted in a deafening roar, their cheers a
validation of Jake's reckless victory. Jake, his features
radiating a mixture of triumph and relief, raised his fist in the air, accepting the adulation with a self-assured swagger.

But the cheers faded into a hollow echo for Riley. The victory was a bittersweet victory, a hollow triumph. He watched as Jake celebrated, his own heart heavy with the weight of their shattered friendship.

The following days were a blur of interviews, media
appearances, and sponsor obligations. The pressure on Jake intensified as he basked in the glow of his recent win, his mind already consumed by the upcoming race. The

celebration had masked a growing unease, a creeping sense of dread that overshadowed his victory.

He could not shake the feeling that his win had come at a terrible price, that he had crossed a line that could not be uncrossed. The weight of his actions, the betrayal he had inflicted, was beginning to consume him, chipping away at his confidence and his composure. The camaraderie he once shared with Riley, the mutual respect that had been the foundation of their friendship, felt like a distant memory, a fragile illusion that had shattered under the strain of his ambition.

The tension within the team was palpable, the air thick with unspoken accusations and resentment. The whispers of Jake's betrayal, the doubts about his motives, had grown louder, the whispers turning into a deafening roar.

One evening, after a grueling day of practice, Jake found himself alone in his hotel room. He sat on the edge of the bed, staring at the flickering television, a silent witness to the emptiness that had become his life. The weight of his deceit, the shattered trust he had left in his wake, was a crushing burden, an unwelcome guest that had taken up permanent residence in his heart.

As he stared at the television screen, a faint knocking on the door startled him. He got up and opened the door to find Riley standing there, his expression grim and his eyes filled with a profound disappointment.

"We need to talk," Riley said, his voice strained.

Jake, his heart sinking, felt a cold wave of fear wash over him. He realized, with a terrible certainty, that he had reached a breaking point, a point where his relentless pursuit of victory had left him standing alone, isolated and drowning in the aftermath of his own actions.

He had pushed his limits, both on the track and in his relationships. His ambition, once a guiding star, had become a destructive force, tearing apart the lives of those closest to him. He had gambled, and he had won, but the victory had come at an unimaginable cost.

The weight of his betrayal hung heavy in the air, a silent condemnation that echoed in the emptiness of his victory. He had tasted the sweet allure of victory, but the taste of it had left a bitter aftertaste, a reminder that the cost of winning can be far more devastating than the thrill of it.

THE RIVALRY PEAKS

The air hung thick with anticipation, a palpable tension that vibrated through the grandstands and onto the asphalt of the dirt track. The smell of burning rubber and gasoline mingled with the scent of popcorn and hot dogs, a symphony of
sights and sounds that pulsed with the very essence of dirt track racing. Tonight was the final race of the season, a
showdown for the championship that promised to rewrite the rules of the game and reshape the lives of everyone involved.

Underneath the glare of the stadium lights, the drivers huddled in their pits, each a storm brewing in their own right. There was Jake "The Hammer" Harrison, the reigning champion, a man known for his ruthless aggression on the track and his icy demeanor off it. His eyes, narrowed under the brim of his cap, held the steely glint of a predator sizing up its prey. Opposite him stood Danny "The Cyclone" Carter, a young upstart with a daring driving style and a fire in his belly that burned brighter than the stadium lights.

Their rivalry had been a simmering cauldron of tension all season long, fuelled by a shared hunger for victory and a deep-seated disdain for one another. It had started as a clash of egos, a battle for supremacy on the track, but it had
spiraled into something darker, a personal vendetta

fueled by whispers of deceit, accusations of sabotage, and the
simmering rage that only a life lived at 100 miles per hour could produce.

The crowd, a cacophony of roaring engines and screaming fans, seemed to sense the weight of this final race. The tension was so thick, you could practically cut it with a knife. The anticipation was electric, a charge crackling through the air, waiting for the spark that would ignite the chaos.

As the drivers lined up on the starting grid, their cars engines thrumming like restless hearts, the weight of the moment pressed down on them. The checkered flag, a symbol of triumph and glory, hung suspended above them, a tangible representation of the prize at stake. This was not just a race; it was a battle for legacy, a fight to cement their names in the annals of dirt track history.

With the drop of the green flag, the world exploded into motion. The roar of the engines, a primal scream, shook the very foundation of the grandstands. The cars, specks of color against the dark asphalt, surged forward, a blur of motion, the air thick with the smell of burning rubber and the whine of tires.

Danny, with his signature audacious style, charged into the lead, a streak of lightning cutting through the pack. Jake, however, was not one to be easily overtaken. He hung back, a predator stalking its prey, waiting for the perfect moment to strike. He knew Danny's aggressive style had its vulnerabilities, and he was patiently waiting for the opportunity to exploit them.

The race was a brutal dance, a ballet of aggression and strategy, a test of skill and endurance. The cars swerved, bumped, and jostled, each driver pushing the limits of their machines and their own bodies. The tension mounted with each passing lap, the air thickening with the smell of burnt rubber and the rumble of engines.

As the laps ticked down, Danny began to show the strain of his relentless pace. He was pushing his car to its limits, the engine screaming in protest. Jake, ever the opportunist, sensed his weakness and moved in for the kill. He made a daring pass, squeezing past Danny on a tight turn, his car a whirlwind of dust and grit.

Danny, unwilling to surrender, fought back with the ferocity of a cornered animal. He matched Jake's every move, his car a blur of color as he tried to regain the lead. The crowd, on their feet, roared with each passing moment, their cheers and jeers echoing through the stadium.

But Danny's luck ran out. On the final lap, he misjudged a turn, sending his car into a dangerous slide. The crowd gasped as his car careened towards the wall, a horrifying spectacle of metal and destruction. The sound of screeching tires echoed through the stadium as Danny wrestled with the car, trying to regain control.

In a moment of sheer brilliance, he managed to straighten the car, but the damage was done. He crossed the finish line in second place, his face a mask of disappointment and frustration. Jake, with a calculated smile on his face, took the checkered flag, his victory a testament to his ruthless strategy and unwavering focus.

As Jake climbed out of his car, the crowd erupted in a mixed chorus of cheers and jeers. His victory, however, was bittersweet. He had won the championship, but at a cost. The image of Danny's near-fatal accident, the look of pain and defeat on his face, haunted Jake. He had won, but at what price?

The aftermath of the race was a whirlwind of emotions. Danny, shaken but alive, emerged from the wreckage, his car a mangled carcass. He was met with a mixture of concern and admiration, the crowd realizing the depth of his courage and skill. Jake, on the other hand, was greeted with a mixture of congratulations and contempt. He had won the championship, but he had also lost something vital – his respect, his honor, and a part of his soul.

The rivalry between Jake and Danny had reached its zenith, leaving an indelible mark on both of them. They had pushed each other to the brink, exposing their vulnerabilities and testing the limits of their endurance. The race had been a battle for victory, a fight for dominance, but it had also been a journey of self-discovery, a confrontation with their inner demons, and a painful realization of the true cost of
ambition.

UNEXPECTED ALLIES

The air hung thick with the smell of burnt rubber and gasoline, a potent cocktail that had become as familiar to the drivers as the scent of their own sweat. The grandstands were packed, a sea of faces illuminated by the flickering lights of the track. The roar of engines was a symphony of power, a guttural roar that pulsed through the very ground beneath their feet. It was a night for heroes, for the drivers who dared to push their machines and themselves to the absolute limit.

The tension was palpable, a silent force that hung heavy in the air. It was more than just the excitement of the race; it was the weight of personal stakes, the pressure of rivalries that ran deeper than any checkered flag.

In the midst of the chaos, there was a simmering undercurrent of something unexpected, a fragile alliance forming amidst the wreckage of fractured connections. It all began with a collision, a brutal impact that sent shockwaves through the pack. Two drivers, Jake "The Hammer" Maddox and Ryan "The Renegade" Carter, found themselves
entangled in a tangle of twisted metal. The incident was a microcosm of their relationship, a long-standing rivalry that had simmered for years, fueled by ambition, jealousy, and a healthy dose of disdain.

But as the dust settled, they realized that the enemy

wasn't each other. It was the shadowy figure lurking on the fringes of the racing world, a manipulator named "The Raven" who had orchestrated the collision, his motivations shrouded in mystery. The Raven's motives were as opaque as his identity, but one thing was clear: he sought to exploit the chaos and turmoil for his own gain.

Jake and Ryan, their anger simmering beneath the surface, found a common ground in their shared mistrust of The Raven. A fragile understanding bloomed in the aftermath of the crash, fueled by a shared desire for vengeance and a need to protect themselves from a force that threatened to
consume them both. It was a fragile alliance, forged in the heat of the moment, but it was a necessary one.

The Raven, however, was a master of manipulation, a
puppeteer who knew how to exploit the weaknesses of his targets. He played on their fears, their insecurities, their desires for revenge, turning them against each other, even as he pulled the strings from behind the scenes.

Their alliance was not without its cracks. The animosity between Jake and Ryan ran deep, the memories of past conflicts and accusations still fresh in their minds. But the threat of The Raven, the looming shadow of his insidious manipulations, forced them to put aside their differences. It was a reluctant truce, but it was the only way to survive.

They began to strategize, whispering in hushed tones,
exchanging information in secret, their movements shrouded in shadows. Their goal was simple: expose The Raven, unravel his web of lies, and bring him down. They sought out unlikely allies, individuals who had been burned by The Raven, who had tasted the bitterness of his manipulation.
They were a ragtag bunch, a collection of wounded souls, each with their own score to settle.

Their plan was daring, risky, a high-stakes game of cat and mouse played out on the racetrack. It was a gamble, a
desperate attempt to reclaim their lives, their destinies, from

the clutches of a man who sought to control their every move.

They needed to expose The Raven's hand, to pull back the curtain and reveal the puppeteer behind the scenes. It was a task fraught with danger, a perilous journey into the heart of a conspiracy that ran deeper than they could have imagined.

One by one, they began to unravel the pieces of the puzzle, piecing together the clues like fragments of a shattered mirror. They discovered that The Raven was not simply a rogue gambler, but a master strategist, a puppet master whose reach extended far beyond the racetrack. He had infiltrated the racing world, manipulating the players like pawns in a game of high stakes, his motives shrouded in darkness.

The stakes were higher than ever before, their lives hanging in the balance. They were forced to confront their own demons, to face the consequences of their choices.

The road ahead was treacherous, but they had found a glimmer of hope in the midst of the chaos. They had found allies, unlikely though they may be, and together they were determined to fight for their future.

It was a battle for control, a fight for their very survival, and they were ready to wage war.

THE FALLOUT

The air hung heavy with the scent of burnt rubber and gasoline, the silence a stark contrast to the deafening roar that had just subsided. The checkered flag had waved, ending the race, but the reverberations of the brutal collision that had punctuated its finish still pulsed in the hearts of those who had witnessed it. The crash had been a spectacle of mangled metal and flying debris, a jarring spectacle that left everyone breathless.

But as the dust settled and the crowd dispersed, the true impact of the incident began to reveal itself. The cheers of victory had died down, replaced by a chilling silence that carried the weight of uncertainty. The tension, thick as smoke, hung over the pit lanes, a palpable sense of unease that permeated the air.

The driver at the center of the crash, the notorious Ace "The Hammer" Lawson, had been miraculously unscathed. He emerged from the wreckage, his face a mask of fury and disbelief, his usual swagger replaced by a chilling calm. The damage to his car, a testament to the force of the impact, was an unsettling reminder of the fragility of his ambition. His eyes, usually gleaming with the fire of a competitor, were now cold, reflecting the harsh realities of the sport he so desperately loved.

Ace's rival, the up-and-coming young sensation, Johnny "The Flash" Carter, had not been so lucky. His car, twisted and crumpled, sat like a mangled carcass in the middle of the track. The silence after the crash was deafening, punctuated only by the rhythmic whine of the rescue crew's sirens.

Johnny's fate hung in the balance, the extent of his injuries shrouded in uncertainty.

As the medical team swarmed around Johnny's mangled car, Ace stood on the sidelines, a distant observer to the unfolding drama. His usual swagger was replaced by a haunted stillness, the fire of competition replaced by a deep-seated fear that gnawed at his conscience.

The impact of the crash had been far greater than just mangled metal and shattered dreams. It had cracked the foundation of the racing world, exposing the raw vulnerability beneath the surface of the sport. The adrenaline rush, the thrill of victory, the roar of the crowd – all faded into insignificance in the face of the sobering reality of risk, loss, and the fragility of life.

The camaraderie that had once united the racing community was now fractured by suspicion and uncertainty. The incident had forced everyone to confront the darker side of their shared passion, to acknowledge the dangerous potential of their reckless pursuit of glory.

The whispers started first, insidious and persistent. They slithered through the pit lanes, fueling speculation and resentment. Some whispered of sabotage, of deliberate intent to cripple Johnny's career. Others suggested a reckless gamble, a desperate move by Ace to gain a decisive edge.

The whispers soon turned into accusations, as tempers flared and old rivalries reignited. The pit lane, once a hub of camaraderie and shared enthusiasm, became a battlefield where accusations flew like poisoned darts. The collision had awakened the demons of suspicion and animosity, turning the racing community into a viper's nest.

The news of the crash sent shockwaves through the racing community, reaching beyond the dirt track, into the hearts of those who had long admired Johnny's talent and Ace's unrelenting spirit. The incident, a grim reminder of the dangers inherent in their sport, left everyone grappling with the uncomfortable truth that racing was not just about speed and skill, but a perilous dance with fate.

The whispers surrounding the crash soon caught the attention of the media, amplifying the tension and fueling speculation. The racing world, once basking in the glory of its heroes, was now under the harsh scrutiny of a public demanding answers.

In the midst of the unfolding chaos, the authorities initiated an investigation into the incident, seeking to uncover the truth behind the crash. They interviewed witnesses, analyzed footage, and meticulously scrutinized the wreckage. The investigation, a painstaking process, became a battleground for truth, justice, and redemption.

Ace, the man who had once reveled in the limelight, now found himself under a microscope, his every move scrutinized, his every statement analyzed. The investigation became a test of his character, a crucible where he would be forced to confront the consequences of his actions.

The weight of the accusations, the pressure of public scrutiny, and the uncertainty surrounding Johnny's condition, all combined to create a perfect storm in Ace's life. The thrill of victory, the intoxicating feeling of power, the adrenaline rush of the race - all faded in the face of the harsh reality of his situation.

He had always lived on the edge, pushing his limits, defying the odds. But now, faced with the possibility of losing it all, he found himself staring into the abyss of his own mortality. The crash, a catalyst for introspection, forced him to confront the depths of his ambition, the price he had paid, and the consequences he now faced.

The investigation was a slow burn, a relentless pursuit of truth that chipped away at the façade of Ace's carefully crafted image. He had always been a master of deception, manipulating the media and his rivals, building a persona that masked the turmoil within. But now, stripped bare, he found himself facing the consequences of his actions.

The pressure mounted, the strain of the investigation slowly eroding his composure. The whispers that had initially haunted him now echoed in his dreams, turning his nights into a waking nightmare. The constant scrutiny, the
relentless pursuit of truth, chipped away at his resolve, revealing the man behind the mask.

As the investigation reached its climax, Ace found himself cornered, his carefully crafted image shattered, his reputation hanging by a thread. The crash, a jarring reminder of the fragility of his dreams, forced him to confront the
consequences of his ambition, the darkness that lurked within his soul.

The collision, a catalyst for introspection, awakened a dormant sense of self-awareness in Ace. He began to see the wreckage of his life, the damage he had inflicted, not just on his rivals, but on himself. The crash, a turning point, not only shattered his dreams but also cracked open his carefully constructed façade, revealing the man behind the mask.

The investigation, a painstaking and relentless pursuit

of truth, forced Ace to confront the demons that had haunted him for years. He had always been a master of deception, a skilled manipulator who played the game by his own rules. But now, stripped bare, he found himself facing the consequences of his actions.

The weight of the accusations, the relentless scrutiny of the media, and the uncertainty surrounding Johnny's fate, all converged to create a perfect storm in Ace's life. He had always lived on the edge, pushing his limits, defying the odds, but now, facing the possibility of losing it all, he found himself staring into the abyss.

The crash, a stark reminder of the fragility of his dreams, forced him to confront the darkness that lurked within his soul. The thrill of victory, the intoxicating feeling of power, the adrenaline rush of the race – all faded in the face of the harsh reality of his situation.

The investigation, a slow burn, a relentless pursuit of truth, chipped away at the façade of Ace's carefully crafted image. He had always been a master of deception, manipulating the media and his rivals, building a persona that masked the turmoil within. But now, stripped bare, he found himself facing the consequences of his actions.

The pressure mounted, the strain of the investigation slowly eroding his composure. The whispers that had initially haunted him now echoed in his dreams, turning his nights into a waking nightmare. The constant scrutiny, the
relentless pursuit of truth, chipped away at his resolve, revealing the man behind the mask.

As the investigation reached its climax, Ace found himself cornered, his carefully crafted image shattered, his reputation hanging by a thread. The crash, a jarring reminder of the fragility of his dreams, forced him to confront the consequences of his ambition, the darkness that lurked within his soul.

The collision, a catalyst for introspection, awakened a dormant sense of self-awareness in Ace. He began to see the wreckage of his life, the damage he had inflicted, not just on his rivals, but on himself. The crash, a turning point, not only shattered his dreams but also cracked open his carefully constructed façade, revealing the man behind the mask.

The investigation, a painstaking and relentless pursuit of truth, forced Ace to confront the demons that had haunted him for years. He had always been a master of deception, a skilled manipulator who played the game by his own rules.
But now, stripped bare, he found himself facing the consequences of his actions.

The weight of the accusations, the relentless scrutiny of the media, and the uncertainty surrounding Johnny's fate, all converged to create a perfect storm in Ace's life. He had always lived on the edge, pushing his limits, defying the odds, but now, facing the possibility of losing it all, he found himself staring into the abyss.

The crash, a stark reminder of the fragility of his dreams, forced him to confront the darkness that lurked within his soul. The thrill of victory, the intoxicating feeling of power, the adrenaline rush of the race – all faded in the face of the harsh reality of his situation.

A SHATTERED ILLUSION

The air hung heavy with the scent of gasoline and burnt rubber, the night sky a canvas of swirling dust and headlight beams. The roar of the engines had died down, leaving a symphony of coughs and sputtering as the cars idled, the drivers slumped in their seats, their bodies vibrating with a residue of adrenaline. The crowd, a sea of faces illuminated by the stadium lights, was a mix of exhilaration and
disappointment, their cheers and jeers a chaotic chorus echoing through the stands.

In the pit lane, a scene of organized chaos unfolded. Crew members scurried around, their faces etched with fatigue, their movements almost balletic in their familiarity. They checked tire pressures, refueled engines, and patted the hood of their cars with a possessive touch, as if they were soothing a wounded animal.

Among the drivers, the atmosphere was thick with tension. They sat in their cars, their faces a mask of exhaustion and frustration. The weight of the race, the pressure of the competition, the disappointment of defeat, or the elation of victory - it all pressed down on them, suffocating them in a suffocating cloak of emotions.

Ethan, his face etched with the grimace of a man who

had just wrestled a wild beast, emerged from his car. The roar of the crowd faded into a muffled hum, replaced by the
rhythmic pounding of his heart. He had won, but the victory tasted like ashes in his mouth. The race had been a blur of adrenaline and fear, the track a canvas of blurred colors and fleeting images. He had pushed himself beyond his limits,

and he could feel the strain in every muscle, the fatigue seeping into his bones.

He scanned the pit lane, his eyes searching for Sarah. Her face, with its sharp cheekbones and fire-red hair, was a familiar beacon in this chaotic world. He needed her, her touch, her soothing presence. He needed her to remind him that he was still alive, that he wasn't just a cog in this
ruthless machine.

He saw her in the distance, her face a mask of concern. She approached him, her steps deliberate, her eyes filled with a silent question. She knew he wasn't alright, just as he knew that she wasn't alright either. The cost of their ambitions, the price of their dreams, was becoming painfully evident. The world of dirt track racing, once a haven of freedom and adrenaline, was starting to feel like a cage, their lives a series of compromises and sacrifices. The victories felt hollow, the defeats devastating.

The night air was filled with the scent of burnt rubber and spilled beer, a bitter cocktail of dreams and reality. The world outside the track, with its demands and pressures, felt like a distant echo, a faded memory. Here, in the realm of dirt and grit, the only reality was the next race, the next victory.

The victories felt like a cruel joke, a fleeting moment of glory that only intensified the gnawing emptiness that
lingered beneath the surface. Ethan had sacrificed everything for this dream - his relationships, his health, his sanity. He had become a prisoner of his own ambitions, trapped in a cycle of relentless pursuit that seemed to offer no respite.

Sarah, standing beside him, was the only constant in his life, the one anchor that kept him grounded. Yet, even she was beginning to feel the strain. The toll of his ambition, the cost of his obsession, was taking its toll on their relationship. They were on a path that led them further away from each other, each step a testament to their shared dreams and their increasingly divergent realities.

The crowd thinned, the lights dimmed, and the cheers faded into a hushed silence. Ethan and Sarah stood in the shadows, the weight of their shared dreams and shattered illusions pressing down on them. They knew they were at a
crossroads, a point where their destinies would diverge, where the cost of their ambitions would become impossible to ignore.

CHAPTER 4: THE BREAKING POINT

The tension in the pit lane was palpable. It was a tangible force, a thick fog that hung in the air, clinging to every surface, suffocating everyone within its reach. The drivers, their faces a mask of hardened determination, were like caged animals, pacing restlessly, their eyes narrowed, their bodies taut with suppressed energy. The crew members, their movements were like clockwork, precise and efficient, their faces etched with an unyielding focus. They were all caught in the eye of a storm, each man and woman aware that the race ahead would change everything.

Ethan sat in his car, his hands clenched around the steering wheel, his body tense, his mind racing. The roar of the engines, the smell of gasoline, the feel of the vibration through his body – all of it was a symphony of adrenaline and anticipation. He was ready. He had to be. The stakes were higher than ever, the competition fiercer, the pressure more intense. This race was a fight for survival, a last stand against the encroaching reality of their ambitions. His world had become a narrow tunnel, a single-minded pursuit of glory and redemption, and there was no turning back.

Sarah, her face a mask of concern, approached him. He could see the doubt in her eyes, the lingering fear of the price he was paying for his relentless pursuit. He wished he could reassure her, tell her it was all going to be okay, but the truth was, he didn't know. The world he was living in, the world he was chasing, was shrouded in uncertainty and danger.

"Ethan, are you sure about this?" Her voice was soft, a whisper in the din of the pit lane.

He met her gaze, his eyes cold and distant. "I have to do this, Sarah. It's everything."

His words were a facade, a desperate attempt to convince himself as much as her. He was scared, terrified of the consequences, the potential for devastation, but he couldn't stop. He had come too far, sacrificed too much, to turn back now.

"Ethan, don't do this. It's not worth it. This is a race, not a war."

His heart ached at the sight of the fear in her eyes, the desperate plea in her voice. He knew she was right. But he had to do this, for himself, for his father, for everyone who had believed in him. This race was his redemption, his chance to prove himself, to finally earn the respect he so desperately craved. He had to win, no matter the cost.

"I know, Sarah. But I have to do this. I have to finish what I started."

He pulled away from her, his gaze fixed on the track, his mind already racing ahead, strategizing, calculating, pushing aside the fear that gnawed at him. He felt Sarah's hand reach out, her fingers brushing his arm, but he didn't turn back. He had to be focused, laser-sharp, if he wanted to survive this race. He needed to win, to prove himself. It was the only way.

The green flag dropped, and the roar of the engines filled the air. Ethan's car lurched forward, the tires screaming in
protest as they grasped the track. The world narrowed, the noise intensified, the air thickened, until all that remained was the blur of colors, the relentless pursuit of the checkered flag. He was a man possessed, his mind consumed by the primal instinct to win, to survive. He pushed his car to its limits, the engine screaming in protest, the tires squealing, the bodywork straining under the pressure. He pushed
himself to his limit, his body aching, his mind racing. His life had become a whirlwind of adrenaline and desperation, a desperate gamble for glory. He was racing against the clock, against the tide, against himself.

The race was a blur of flashing lights and screeching tires, a chaotic symphony of metal and muscle. Ethan, his hands gripping the steering wheel, his body taut with tension, navigated the track with a skill honed over years of practice and sacrifice. He was in his element, the asphalt beneath him a familiar friend, the roar of the engine a comforting
companion. The pressure, the competition, the danger – it was all exhilarating.

He was losing himself in the race, his mind consumed by the pursuit of victory, his body responding to the demands of the machine. He was a warrior, a gladiator in the arena of asphalt and adrenaline. He was fighting for his life, for his legacy, for his place in history.

But the race was not a solitary pursuit. It was a battleground, a collision of ambition and desperation, of dreams and realities. The other drivers, their faces twisted in a mix of determination and aggression, were his adversaries, his rivals, his enemies. They were all fighting for the same prize, the same elusive glory, and they were all willing to do anything to win.

The competition was fierce, the rivalries intense, and the tension was a palpable force that hung in the air, threatening to explode. The race was a test of skill, strategy, and resilience. It was a game of cat and mouse, of calculated risks and unexpected twists. It was a world where the rules were fluid, the lines blurred, and the stakes were always high.

As the laps ticked by, the pressure mounted, the tension tightened, and the race became a desperate struggle for survival. Ethan, his body weary, his mind strained, his heart pounding, pushed himself to his limits. He was fighting against the odds, against the tide, against himself. He was fighting to win, but he was also fighting to stay alive.

The race had become a symbol of their lives, their choices, their sacrifices. They were all racing against the clock, against the tide, against the relentless march of time. They were all searching for something, something elusive and undefined, something that would validate their existence, give their lives meaning, and leave behind a legacy that would outlive them.

The checkered flag waved, signaling the end of the race, and the crowd erupted in a frenzy of cheers and jeers. Ethan, his body exhausted, his mind drained, his heart pounding, pulled his car to a stop. He had won. He had triumphed. He had achieved his goal.

But as he climbed out of his car, the weight of his victory pressed down on him. The cheers of the crowd, the roar of the engines, the adrenaline coursing through his veins – it all felt hollow, distant, irrelevant. He had achieved victory, but at what cost? He had won the race, but he had lost himself.

He looked for Sarah in the crowd, her face a blur in the sea of faces, her presence a distant echo in the cacophony of noise. He wanted to tell her about the race, about the victory, about the triumph. But he couldn't. The words stuck in his throat, choked by the realization of the emptiness that lay beneath the surface. He had won the race, but he had lost her.

He turned away from the crowd, his steps heavy, his shoulders slumped, his mind racing. He had to find Sarah, to tell her how he felt, to confess his guilt, to apologize for his relentless pursuit. He had to tell her the truth. The truth was that he had won the race, but he had lost everything else. He had lost his soul.

PICKING UP THE PIECES

The air hung heavy with the lingering scent of burnt rubber and diesel, a pungent reminder of the chaos that had
unfolded just days before. The grandstand, once a sea of roaring fans, stood silent, a testament to the abrupt end of the racing season. The track, usually a canvas of vibrant colors and swirling dust, now lay bare, its surface scarred from the battles fought upon it. The dust had settled, but the echoes of the final race reverberated through the lives of the drivers and crew, etching their mark on each of them.

For many, the season's conclusion had been a brutal reckoning. Their dreams of glory lay in ruins, shattered by the unforgiving nature of the sport. The pursuit of the checkered flag had left them wounded, emotionally and physically, bearing the weight of broken promises and shattered ambitions. The deafening roar of the engines had faded, replaced by the quiet murmurs of remorse and the gnawing ache of what could have been.

But within the wreckage of shattered dreams, a flicker of hope began to ignite. The darkness that had shrouded the racing community began to recede, revealing a glimmer of a new dawn. The characters who had been consumed by the whirlwind of competition, their lives turned upside down by the relentless pursuit of victory, started to pick up the pieces of their lives.

For Jake, the reigning champion, the season's end brought a different kind of reckoning. His victory had come at a heavy cost, a price he was now forced to confront. His triumph had been tainted by the shadows of his past, his deceitful actions leaving him isolated and haunted by the weight of his guilt.

His once-unwavering confidence was replaced by a deep-seated unease, a constant reminder of the fragility of his accomplishments. He had tasted the sweetness of victory, only to discover that it was a bitter pill, leaving a residue of unease on his tongue.

The weight of his actions pressed upon him, forcing him to confront the truth he had so desperately tried to bury. He realized that his relentless pursuit of the checkered flag had driven him to a precipice, a point where he had compromised his integrity and endangered the lives of others. He had used his talent and skill to manipulate and deceive, his ambition eclipsing his sense of right and wrong. The truth, once suppressed, now clawed its way to the surface, threatening to unravel the carefully constructed facade he had created.

Yet, within this dark abyss of self-doubt, a flicker of hope emerged. He saw the pain he had inflicted on those closest to him, the wounds he had opened, and he felt a yearning for redemption. The guilt that had been a constant companion now transformed into a catalyst for change. He recognized the need to make amends, to repair the damage he had caused. The fire of ambition that had consumed him began to dim, replaced by a newfound understanding of the true value of genuine relationships and unwavering integrity.

For Alex, the young and ambitious driver who had been Jake's rival throughout the season, the ending had brought a sense of disillusionment. His dreams of becoming a champion had been shattered, the realization that his path to glory was paved with deceit and betrayal leaving him feeling betrayed and lost. He had been blinded by the allure of success, his desire to surpass Jake pushing him to the edge of ethical boundaries.

The weight of his choices bore down on him, a constant reminder of the path he had chosen. He had embraced the tactics that had driven him to the top, ignoring the whispers of conscience that warned him of the dangerous path he was forging. His ambition had consumed him, driving him to prioritize winning at all costs. He had become a product of the environment he inhabited, mirroring the cutthroat competition that defined the world of dirt track racing.

As he looked back on the season, he realized that his victory, however hollow, had come at a steep price. He had sacrificed his integrity, his reputation, and his friendships in the pursuit of glory. The weight of his actions felt like a leaden chain around his neck, dragging him down into the abyss of regret.
He saw his reflection in the shattered pieces of his dreams, realizing that his quest for glory had been fueled by a thirst for validation that remained unquenched.

But within the ashes of his shattered dreams, a spark of hope ignited. The sting of defeat had forced him to confront the truth of his choices, revealing the emptiness at the heart of his pursuits. The realization of his mistakes ignited a desire for change, a yearning for redemption. He knew he couldn't turn back time, but he could choose a different path, one paved with honesty, integrity, and genuine connections.

For Mary, the lone woman in the tight-knit community of racers, the season's end had brought a sense of liberation. She had spent years fighting for recognition, battling against the prejudice that permeated the sport. She had been forced to prove herself again and again, her talent overshadowed by the biases of the world she inhabited.

The season had been a testament to her resilience, her unwavering determination a beacon of hope amidst the darkness. She had defied expectations, proving that talent and skill transcended gender barriers. But the victory came at a personal cost, the relentless pursuit of her dreams pushing her to the edge of exhaustion.

She realized that her drive to succeed had been fueled by a desire to break free from the shackles of societal expectations. She had sought validation not only from the racing community but also from herself. She had battled against the winds of doubt, her every race a statement of defiance against the world that tried to confine her.

The season's end brought a sense of weariness but also a sense of accomplishment. She had overcome the odds, proving herself in a world that had never truly believed in her. Her journey had been marked by both triumphs and tribulations, her resolve tested at every turn. She had faced down the demons of self-doubt, emerging from the crucible of adversity stronger and more determined than ever before.

The season's end brought a sense of closure, a chance to reflect on the path she had traveled. Her journey had been marked by moments of exhilaration and despair, but she had emerged from the crucible of competition with her spirit unbroken. The memories of the battles she had fought, the challenges she had overcome, now served as a source of strength and inspiration. Her heart was heavy with the burden of the past, but it also brimmed with a sense of hope for the future.

The racing community was left in a state of flux, their world turned upside down by the events of the past season. The lines between ambition and integrity, loyalty and betrayal, had been blurred, leaving them reeling from the consequences of their actions. The camaraderie that had once defined them had been tested and broken, leaving them questioning their values and questioning their place within this unforgiving world.

But in the aftermath of the season, a sense of resilience began to emerge. The drivers and crew, faced with the wreckage of their past, started to rebuild their lives. The shared experiences they had endured, the trials they had faced, forged a bond that transcended the divisions that had threatened to tear them apart.

The dust settled, leaving behind a landscape scarred by the battles of the past season. The roar of the engines faded, replaced by the murmur of reflection and the whispers of hope. The world of dirt track racing, a world built on speed and competition, was slowly transforming, adapting to the changing tides of time. The pursuit of the checkered flag, once an all-consuming obsession, was replaced by a desire for something more.

The drivers and crew, now stripped bare of their illusions, were left to confront the consequences of their actions. They had been forced to face the truth of their choices, the flaws that lay beneath their carefully constructed facades. They had tasted victory, only to discover that it was a bitter pill, leaving a residue of unease on their tongues.

The season had ended, but the journey was far from over. The racing world, a world built on speed, ambition, and unwavering determination, was poised for a new beginning. The drivers and crew, scarred by the battles of the past, were ready to face the future. They had learned from their
mistakes, their hearts now open to the possibility of redemption, their spirits yearning for a new dawn.

The world of dirt track racing, with its

intoxicating blend of speed, danger, and passion, had forever changed them. They had seen the darkness that lurked beneath the surface, the relentless pursuit of glory that could consume even the most seasoned competitor. They had been through hell and back, their lives forever intertwined by the shared experiences they had endured.

As they looked to the horizon, they saw a new dawn, a promise of a brighter future. The racing world was still out there, waiting to be conquered. But they knew, with a newfound clarity, that the path ahead was not about chasing the checkered flag at all costs. It was about embracing the values of integrity, compassion, and genuine connection. It was about recognizing that the true victory lay not in winning, but in the journey itself. The race continues, but for these drivers and crew, the stakes had changed. The pursuit of glory had given way to a desire for something more, a desire for a future built on honesty and redemption.

REDEMPTION AND FORGIVENESS

The dust had settled on the tumultuous season, leaving behind a trail of broken dreams, shattered alliances, and a chilling emptiness that lingered in the air. The roar of the engines had faded into a distant memory, replaced by the quiet hum of reflection and the weight of decisions made in the heat of the moment. The racetrack, once a stage for triumph and defeat, now stood as a stark reminder of the consequences of unchecked ambition and the enduring power of forgiveness.

For some, the end of the season brought a sense of relief, a chance to escape the relentless pressure and scrutiny. For others, it was a time of reckoning, a period for confronting the demons of their past and seeking redemption amidst the wreckage. The lines between victor and vanquished blurred, as the weight of actions taken and words spoken echoed in the silence.

Among those grappling with the aftermath was Jake "The Hammer" Miller, the driver whose meteoric rise to fame was marred by a reckless streak that had cost him dearly. His victory in the championship race had been tainted by a

ruthless maneuver that had sent his closest rival, the veteran driver, Danny "The Ghost" Thompson, crashing into the wall. The move had sparked outrage and condemnation, with accusations of deliberate sabotage swirling around Jake. He had won the title, but at a heavy price.

The incident had fractured the fragile trust that had once bound Jake and Danny together. Their rivalry, once fueled by mutual respect and a shared passion for the sport, had descended into a bitter feud that threatened to consume them both. Jake, haunted by the memory of Danny's crash, sought solace in the fleeting embrace of victory, but found no comfort in the hollow echoes of his success. He knew he had crossed a line, and the consequences were far-reaching.

The weight of his actions pressed heavily on Jake's conscience. He had witnessed firsthand the devastation that his recklessness had caused, the pain etched on Danny's face as he lay crumpled in the wreckage, the fear that had gripped him as he realized the magnitude of his mistake. The cheers of the crowd faded into a deafening silence as he confronted the true cost of his victory.

Danny, a seasoned driver with a reputation for unwavering integrity, found himself grappling with a betrayal that cut deep. He had trusted Jake, seen a kindred spirit in his relentless pursuit of the checkered flag. But Jake's actions had shattered that trust, leaving him with a sense of disillusionment and a deep-seated resentment that threatened to consume him.

In the wake of the crash, both Jake and Danny found themselves at a crossroads. The path to redemption lay before them, shrouded in the shadows of doubt and uncertainty. For Jake, it was a journey of confronting his demons, acknowledging the pain he had inflicted, and seeking forgiveness from the man he had wronged. For Danny, it was a quest for healing, a chance to rise above the bitterness and reclaim the integrity that had defined him.

The burden of guilt weighed heavily on Jake. He found himself reliving the crash in his nightmares, the sickening thud of metal against metal, the screams of the crowd as they watched in horror. He tried to silence the voices in his head, to escape the torment that consumed him, but the truth had a way of finding its way back. He knew that he had to face Danny, to make amends for the pain he had caused.

The journey to redemption was not a linear path, but a winding road strewn with obstacles and temptations. Jake had to navigate the treacherous landscape of his own demons, the whispers of doubt that tempted him to abandon his quest. The racing world, fueled by ego and ambition, offered him a temporary escape, a chance to drown his guilt in the roar of the engines. But the allure of the track was a fleeting illusion, a temporary fix for a wound that ran deep.

Danny, meanwhile, found solace in the support of his family and the unwavering loyalty of his crew. They offered him strength and encouragement, reminding him of his resilience and the unwavering integrity that had always defined him. But the bitterness of betrayal lingered, a constant reminder of the pain that had been inflicted upon him. He wrestled with his own demons, the temptation to harbor resentment and seek revenge, but the spirit of sportsmanship that had always guided him kept him anchored.

As the days turned into weeks, a sense of urgency gripped Jake. He knew he had to act, to break free from the chains of his guilt. He reached out to Danny, knowing that the road to forgiveness would not be easy, but determined to take the first step.

The encounter was fraught with tension, a collision of emotions that threatened to consume them both. Danny's eyes, once filled with admiration and respect, now reflected a mix of anger and hurt. He listened to Jake's apology, his words heavy with sincerity and regret. But the wounds ran deep, the scars etched by betrayal were not easily erased.

Jake's words resonated with a raw honesty that pierced through Danny's defenses. He saw the genuine remorse in Jake's eyes, the flicker of regret that reflected a struggle for redemption. The weight of his own anger began to ease, replaced by a glimmer of understanding. He knew that Jake's actions had been fueled by desperation, by a thirst for victory that had consumed him.

The forgiveness that Danny offered was not an easy one. It was a conscious decision, a testament to his own strength and the enduring power of hope. He understood that Jake was not a monster, but a man grappling with his own demons. He saw the potential for change, the possibility of redemption.

The process of healing was gradual, a journey of small steps and hard-won victories. Jake, armed with a newfound sense of purpose, committed himself to a path of self-improvement, seeking guidance from mentors and coaches who could help him navigate the treacherous waters of his own ambition. He made amends for his past mistakes, extending his hand to those he had wronged, seeking to rebuild the trust that had been broken.

The road to redemption is rarely a straight one. There were setbacks, moments of doubt, and temptations that threatened to derail Jake's progress. But he persevered, driven by the weight of his past mistakes and the hope of a brighter future.

Danny, too, faced his own challenges. He had to reconcile the pain of betrayal with the enduring spirit of sportsmanship that had always defined him. He had to find a way to move forward, to embrace the future without allowing the bitterness of the past to consume him.

As the seasons turned and the racing world continued to churn, Jake and Danny emerged as unlikely allies. The bond forged in the crucible of forgiveness and redemption was stronger than the rivalries that had once divided them. They found solace in shared experiences, a mutual understanding that transcended the boundaries of the racetrack. Their journey, a testament to the resilience of the human spirit, served as a reminder that even in the darkest depths of despair, hope can find a way to shine.

LESSONS LEARNED

The silence of the empty garage was a stark contrast to the cacophony of the track. The lingering scent of engine oil and burnt rubber hung heavy in the air, a tangible reminder of the brutal season that had just ended. Each clang of a wrench, each hum of the engine hoist, was a jarring echo in the quiet space. I stood there, hands tucked into the pockets of my worn racing jacket, staring at the dismantled car. It was a testament to the relentless pursuit of victory, a mangled monument to the unyielding desire to cross the finish line first.

The season had been a whirlwind of high-speed chases, backstabbing maneuvers, and heart-stopping moments that pushed the limits of both man and machine. I had poured every ounce of my being into it, leaving my sanity, my relationships, and even my physical well-being on the track.
I had pushed myself further than I ever thought possible, testing the boundaries of my endurance and challenging the limits of my skill.

It was a game of inches, a brutal ballet of steel and horsepower. Every turn, every pass, was a calculated risk, a gamble with everything I had. The thrill of the competition was intoxicating, an adrenaline rush that fueled me through the long, grueling hours of training and preparation. But the pressure, the constant fear of failure, the relentless pursuit of perfection, had taken its toll.

As I looked at the dismantled car, I saw the scars of the battle. Bent fenders, cracked chassis, and a dented hood bore witness to the hard-fought victories and crushing defeats.

EACH SCRATCH, EACH DENT, REPRESENTED A MOMENT OF INTENSE

pressure, a split-second decision that had left its mark. But beneath the damage, I saw the beauty of the machine. It was a testament to human ingenuity, a symbol of the unwavering pursuit of speed and dominance.

But the racing world wasn't just about the cars. It was about the people – the drivers, the crews, the sponsors, the fans. It was a microcosm of the human experience, a tapestry woven with threads of ambition, betrayal, loyalty, and love. I had witnessed firsthand the lengths people would go to for victory, the sacrifices they made, the risks they took. I had seen the dark underbelly of the sport, the greed and corruption that lurked beneath the surface.

I had learned about myself, about my own strengths and weaknesses. I had discovered the depths of my own determination and the limits of my resilience. I had faced my own demons, the doubts and insecurities that had shadowed me for so long. The racing world, with its relentless pursuit of victory, had forced me to confront my deepest fears and insecurities. It had exposed the raw, unfiltered truth about myself, leaving me with no place to hide.

The season had taken a heavy toll on me, both physically and emotionally. The constant strain of the competition had pushed me to the brink. I had lost friends, alienated loved ones, and even endangered my own life in the pursuit of glory. But amidst the wreckage, amidst the heartbreak and the pain, I had discovered a sense of purpose, a newfound clarity that had been missing for so long.

The experience had been transformative, a crucible that had forged me into something stronger, more resilient. I had learned the true meaning of sacrifice, the importance of hard work, and the value of perseverance. I had learned that winning was not everything, that the journey was just as important as the destination. And I had learned that the greatest victory was not crossing the finish line first, but facing your fears and overcoming your limitations.

As I stood there, contemplating the wreckage of the season, I realized that the true test was not in the race itself, but in the aftermath. It was about picking up the pieces, healing the wounds, and learning from the mistakes. It was about facing the consequences of my actions, taking responsibility for my choices, and moving forward with a renewed sense of purpose.

The road ahead was uncertain, but I was no longer the same man who had stepped onto the track at the start of the season. I had been tested, I had been broken, but I had also been reborn. The racing world had taught me lessons that would stay with me for a lifetime, lessons about resilience, about perseverance, about the human spirit's ability to endure and overcome even the most challenging obstacles. The scars of the season were a reminder of the battles I had fought, the sacrifices I had made, and the lessons I had learned. They were a testament to the journey, a reminder that the real race was not just about crossing the finish line, but about the lessons learned along the way.

A NEW PATH

The dust settled on the final checkered flag of the season. The cacophony of cheers and jeers from the crowd faded as the energy drained from the racetrack, leaving behind a silence that echoed the lingering tension and the weight of what had transpired. For the drivers and crew members who had poured their hearts and souls into this pursuit of glory, the season's end was a bittersweet moment. The thrill of competition had been exhilarating, but the toll it had taken was undeniable.

The air hung heavy with the scent of burnt rubber and gasoline, a lingering testament to the fierce battles waged on the track. The engines had roared their last, their power echoing the passion that fueled their drivers, yet the echoes of those roars now seemed to whisper a different message, one of introspection, of a need to reassess the path that had been so eagerly pursued.

Among those who had poured their heart and soul into the race was Amelia, the fiery driver with a spirit as wild as the car she piloted. She had always believed in the thrill of
competition, believing it fueled her to push beyond her limits. But as the dust settled on the season, she was left with a gnawing sense of unease. Her relentless pursuit of victory had come at a cost, not just in the physical demands of the sport, but in the erosion of the relationships that had once anchored her. She was a shadow of her former self, her fiery spirit dimmed by

the relentless pressure she had imposed upon herself, a pressure that seemed to stem not from the competition itself but from the relentless pursuit of external validation.

In the quiet aftermath of the season's final race, Amelia found herself at a crossroads. The roar of the engines had faded, replaced by a quiet murmur of reflection. She saw the toll her ambition had taken, the sacrifices made, the
relationships strained, and a sense of emptiness that settled in her heart. The victories had felt hollow, the cheers of the crowd a distant echo in the emptiness that now consumed her.

A sense of peace descended on her, as if a storm within her had finally subsided. She understood that her journey had been about more than just winning races. It had been about pushing her limits, discovering her own strength, and finding her place in a world that was both exhilarating and
unforgiving. But in her pursuit of victory, she had lost sight of the simple pleasures that had once brought her joy: the camaraderie of the crew, the thrill of the chase, the
camaraderie of a shared love of speed.

As the sun began to set, casting long shadows across the deserted track, Amelia took a deep breath and felt a surge of clarity. She was not defined by her victories, nor by the accolades she had earned. She was a woman of courage, a woman of resilience, a woman who had learned to embrace the challenges of life, both on and off the track.

In the silence that followed, Amelia resolved to embark on a new path. She would continue to race, but with a renewed sense of purpose, a deeper appreciation for the journey, and a greater understanding of the true meaning of victory. She would race not for validation, but for the joy of the sport, for the camaraderie she had shared, and for the challenges that lay ahead. Her journey, she realized, was just beginning.

Meanwhile, across town, at a dimly lit bar, Jack, a young mechanic with a heart of gold, sat nursing a beer. He had spent years working behind the scenes, his grease-stained hands a testament to his dedication to the sport, and his love for racing a passion he had poured into every bolt tightened, every engine tuned. He had witnessed the highs and lows of the sport, the betrayals and the triumphs, the sacrifices made and the bonds forged. He had poured his heart and soul into the pursuit of victory, but the victory that he sought wasn't the thrill of the checkered flag, but the sense of fulfillment that came with knowing that he had played a part in bringing those victories to fruition.

Jack was a man of few words, but his actions spoke volumes. He was the unsung hero of the track, the backbone of the team, the steady hand in the storm. He had seen the darkness that lurked beneath the glitz and glamour of the racing
world, the greed and ambition that could consume even the most well-intentioned souls. He had seen how victory could turn men into monsters, how the pursuit of glory could leave them broken and empty. He was no stranger to heartache, having seen his own dreams crumble under the weight of disappointment, his own heart broken by the betrayal of those he had trusted.

Yet, even amidst the shadows, Jack had never lost his faith in the good that existed in the world. He believed that true victory lay not in the pursuit of individual glory, but in the bonds of brotherhood, in the camaraderie that transcended competition, in the shared pursuit of a common goal. He saw the beauty in the simplicity of the sport, in the raw passion that fueled the engines, in the dedication of the crew who worked tirelessly behind the scenes. He found solace in the quiet moments of reflection, in the clinking of wrenches, the smell of gasoline, the feeling of cold metal against his hands. He had seen the dark side of racing, but he had also seen the light, the beauty that existed in the heart of the sport, the passion that burned brightly in the eyes of those who loved it.

The bar was a haven for Jack, a place where he could escape the pressures of the track, where he could unwind and reflect on the path that lay ahead. He knew his life was intertwined with the world of racing, that the roar of the engines had become the soundtrack of his existence. But he also knew that the life he had chosen was not without its sacrifices. His time was consumed by the demands of the sport, his life centered around the track. He had chosen to dedicate himself to something bigger than himself, to a world that was both exhilarating and demanding, but he had done so with
unwavering dedication, fueled by a passion that burned as brightly as the engines he helped maintain.

As Jack sat at the bar, contemplating the lessons he had learned, a thought struck him. He had always been content with his life behind the scenes, but a new path was calling to him, a path that would take him out of the shadows and into the light, a path that would allow him to share his passion with others, to mentor the next generation of racers. He had dedicated his life to the world of racing, and he felt a deep sense of purpose in sharing his knowledge with those who were just starting out, in guiding them through the
complexities of the sport, in helping them to find their place in the world of high-speed thrills and dangerous turns.

His heart pounded with anticipation, his mind racing with new possibilities. He knew that the road ahead would be challenging, that there would be obstacles to overcome, but he was ready. He had weathered the storms, learned from his mistakes, and emerged stronger than ever before. He had found his purpose, and he was ready to embrace it, to
dedicate his life to a new generation of racers, to share his

passion, and to help them find their own place in the fast-paced, exhilarating world of dirt track racing.

In the stillness of the night, Jack rose from his barstool, his resolve solidified. He would leave behind the shadows of the pit crew and step into the light, sharing his knowledge and experience, guiding the next generation of racers, and ensuring that the spirit of the sport, the passion that burned so brightly within him, would continue to light the way for those who followed in his footsteps.

THE RACE CONTINUES

The sun dipped below the horizon, casting long shadows across the dirt track as the final checkered flag fell. The air was thick with the scent of burnt rubber and gasoline, a symphony of cheers and jeers echoing through the grandstands. For many, the season had ended, the culmination of months of tireless effort and relentless pursuit of the checkered flag. But for those who had tasted the bitter sting of defeat, the echoes of the engines seemed to carry a different message - a message of unfulfilled ambitions, of dreams left shattered.

The pit lanes buzzed with activity, a whirlwind of mechanics and crew members scrambling to dismantle and pack the cars. The air crackled with tension, a palpable mixture of relief and disappointment hanging heavy in the air. There were congratulations whispered and shared beers, but
mostly, there was a quiet somberness. The thrill of victory and the agony of defeat had woven their magic once again, leaving a tapestry of emotions in their wake.

For Jake, the taste of defeat lingered like a bitter aftertaste. He had come so close, the checkered flag tantalizingly within reach, only to be overtaken in the final lap by his archrival, the ruthless and cunning Riley. The thought of the race replayed in his mind, each turn, each maneuver, each missed opportunity. It was a symphony of what-ifs, a cruel reminder of his failure.

He stood alone in the darkness, his back to the deserted track, the silence broken only by the distant hum of generators. The weight of the loss pressed down on him, a physical manifestation of the shattered dreams. The promise of glory had seemed so close, only to be snatched away in a heart-stopping final lap.

But in the midst of the disillusionment, a spark of resolve ignited within him. It wasn't just about the trophy or the fame, it was about the fire that burned within him, a fire fueled by the challenge, the relentless pursuit of perfection. The roar of the engines was no longer a symphony of defeat, but a haunting reminder of the unfinished symphony, the next chapter waiting to be written.

As he walked away from the track, the echo of the engines faded into the night, leaving only the steady rhythm of his footsteps. The racing world was a relentless beast,
demanding constant evolution, adaptation, and reinvention. This season was just one verse in the ever-evolving story of his life, a chapter closed, but the book was far from finished.

In the bustling pits, his crew was already dismantling the car, preparing it for the long drive home. They were a family, united by their passion for the sport, their shared dreams and disappointments. He knew their disappointment ran as deep as his own, but he also saw the flicker of determination in their eyes, the understanding that this was just a pause, a temporary setback in their pursuit of glory.

The dirt track world was a relentless ecosystem, always evolving, always pushing the boundaries of human potential. There were no guarantees, no shortcuts to success, only endless opportunities for failure and the unyielding determination to rise again.

He looked out at the track, bathed in the pale moonlight, the canvas for a thousand stories. The familiar scent of burnt rubber and gasoline hung in the air, a tangible reminder of the raw, untamed energy that thrummed beneath the surface.

The world of dirt track racing was a crucible, testing every aspect of a man's character, his strength, his resolve, his very soul.

He knew he wouldn't be able to outrun the past, the ghosts of the season's failures. But he also knew that he couldn't be bound by them. He had to find a way to rise from the ashes, to learn from the mistakes, to refine his craft, to come back stronger, faster, more resilient.

The racing world was a world of constant change, of unpredictable twists and turns, of relentless pursuit and unforgiving consequences. But for Jake, it was also a world of possibility, of endless potential, of a future filled with the promise of redemption and the chance to rewrite his story.

He knew that the journey would be long and arduous, filled with challenges and sacrifices. But he also knew that the fire within him, the unyielding passion for the sport, would keep him going. He would come back, not just for the glory, but for the thrill of the chase, the raw, unadulterated adrenaline rush, the test of his mettle against the unforgiving demands of the track.

The next season was just around the corner, and he was ready to face it head-on, with the scars of the past etched on his soul and the unwavering belief in his own potential burning brightly within him.

The world of dirt track racing wasn't for the faint of heart. It demanded a certain kind of grit, a willingness to push beyond the limits of endurance, to embrace the chaos and the uncertainty. It was a world where success was fleeting and failure was ever-present. But it was also a world where the spirit of competition, the relentless pursuit of victory, could bind individuals in ways that defied logic and reason.

For Jake, the journey was far from over. The echoes of the past would remain, a constant reminder of the sacrifices made and the lessons learned. But the future, with its
boundless possibilities, beckoned, urging him forward into the next chapter, the next race, the next challenge. The roar of the engines would be his soundtrack, the dirt track his canvas, and the pursuit of victory his guiding star.

As the engines roared to life in the distant garages, the echoes of the season past gave way to the promise of the season to come. A new dawn was breaking, a new chapter unfolding, and Jake, the man who had tasted defeat, was ready to embrace it.

ACKNOWLEDGMENTS

A story like this doesn't just spring to life from thin air. It takes a village, or at least a few dedicated individuals, to help a writer navigate the treacherous turns and hairpin bends of the creative process. First and foremost, my deepest gratitude goes to the passionate individuals who live and breathe the world of dirt track racing. Your dedication, skill, and grit inspired every word on these pages.

A special thanks to [insert names of individuals who provided specific feedback or support, e.g., technical advisors, beta readers, editors]. Your insights, feedback, and unwavering belief in this project were invaluable.

Finally, to my family and friends, thank you for enduring the late nights, the mumbled plot points, and the occasional outburst of creative frustration. Your love and support are the fuel that keeps me going.

APPENDIX

This appendix provides a glimpse into the technical aspects of dirt track Late Model racing, offering insights into the cars, the tracks, and the rules that govern this high-octane sport.

A.1 The Cars:
Chassis:
[Brief description of the standard chassis used for Late Models, including materials and construction.]
Engine:
[Details about the engine specifications, including displacement, horsepower, and modifications allowed.]
Suspension:
[Explanation of the suspension setup, focusing on the unique aspects of dirt track racing.]
Tires:
[Information about the type of tires used, their construction, and the role of tire pressure in handling.]

A.2 The Tracks:
Surface:
[Description of the dirt track surface, including types of dirt used and track preparation techniques.]
Banking:
[Explanation of the banking angle of the track and how it affects racing lines.]
Layout:
[Information about the typical layout of a dirt track, including the size of the track and the location of the

turns.]

A.3 The Rules:
Safety Regulations:
[Overview of the safety regulations in place to protect drivers and spectators.]
Competition Rules:
[Explanation of the rules governing competition, including penalties for infractions.]
Technical Inspection:
[Description of the technical
inspection process that all cars must undergo before racing.]

GLOSSARY

Banking:
The angle of the track's surface, which is typically sloped towards the inside of the turns.

Bump Draft:
A racing technique where a car uses the air disturbance created by the car in front to gain speed.

Checkered Flag:
The flag waved at the end of a race to signal the winner.

Late Model:
A type of dirt track racing car that is known for its speed and maneuverability.

Pit Stop:
A stop during a race where a car receives fuel, tire changes, and other repairs.

Safety Car:
A vehicle that leads the race under caution, typically after an accident or debris on the track.

Slide Job:
A racing maneuver where a driver moves their car to the outside of another car and then uses the momentum to pass them.

Spin-out:
A loss of control of a car, resulting in a rotation on the track.

Yellow Flag:
A flag waved to signal a caution period during a race.

References

[Insert any relevant sources consulted for research, e.g., books, articles, websites, interviews]

AUTHOR BIOGRAPHY

[Your name] is a seasoned author of gritty, fast-paced thrillers. Driven by a passion for adrenaline-fueled worlds, they have a particular affinity for stories set against
backdrops of racing and crime. Their work is known for its immersive character development, captivating plots, and a sharp focus on the dark side of human nature.

[Optionally, you can include additional details about your writing career, inspirations, or interests.]

Made in United States
Orlando, FL
06 April 2025